Lady Luck

Hugh Wiley

Contents

LADY LUCK

BY

Hugh Wiley

LADY LUCK

By HUGH WILEY

"When you 's travellin' heavy on de misery road
An' yo' back is breakin' wid de misery load,
Jes' figger dat yo' trouble 's boun' to end,
Cause Lady Luck is waitin' fo' you, 'roun de bend."

THE WILDCAT

LADY LUCK
CHAPTER I

Ah wuz a fiel' han' fo' Ah sailed de sea,
Wisht Ah wuz a fiel' han' now.
Dis konk'rin' hero business don' make no hit wid me--
Wisht Ah wuz a fiel' han' now.

"Gimme back a nickel! How come coffee ten cents? Gimme back 'at nickel befo' bofe ob us is on de same side ob de lunch counter."

"You an' a policeman, you means. Ca'm yo'se'f. If dis wah keeps up, coffee g'wine cost fifteen cents nex' week."

"How come wah? Wah finished a yeah back. Me an' Cap'n Jack wuz de fust men in de wah. Wah's done. Ah knows. Gimme back 'at nickel."

"Mebbe de wah is done, but de Democrats ain't. Git out ob heah wid dat goat, fo' you ruins mah trade."

The Wildcat picked up Captain Jack's bed-roll from the floor beside the lunch counter in the Memphis station. He accumulated Lily from where the travelworn mascot goat was tethered to an adjoining stool. Together they walked from the lunch room in which he had sought refreshment after an arduous ride from San Francisco to Memphis.

"Come on heah, Lily. Ol' Cap'n Jack an' de lady done went home in a takes-a-grab. Boy takes a grab at yo' money, an' if deys any lef', you gives it to a policeman fo' arrestin' him. Us rides a 'spress wagon."

On the street fronting the station the Wildcat chartered a rickety express wagon hauled by a languid black mule. "Whuf!" the driver grunted. "Sho' is de ponderestest bed-roll Ah eveh lifted."

"'At bed-roll's full of iron helmets f'm dead Germans, fo' Cap'n Jack to 'membeh de wah by. De officehs craves to 'membeh de wah. Us 'listed boys craves to fo'git it."

The driver of the express wagon looked sideways at the Wildcat. "When did de goat die?"

"How come?"

"Sit him on de side ob me whah de win' ain't blowin'. Wuz he de Dove ob Peace de wah'd go on fo'eveh. Whut's dem culled ribbons doin' on dat goat?"

"De blue ribbon is mah mascot's quality. De red an' white ones is patriotism."

"Thought mebbe dey wuz fus' an' secon' prizes fo' smellin'."

The Wildcat handed the driver of the express wagon a cigar.

"Smoke dis offsetteh," he said. Drifting along on a haze of conflicting aromas, the outfit arrived finally at the residence of Captain Jack. "Heah's de fifty cents," the Wildcat said to the express driver.

"Cost me dat to git de goat smell renovated off me. Wuth six bits."

"On yo' way. I'll six bits you! Quit whiffin' wid dat nose, befo' I busts yo' loose f'm it. On yo' way! C'm on, Lily."

The Wildcat spent the rest of the afternoon shuffling furniture around inside of Captain Jack's house. At four o'clock Captain Jack's wife arrived, convoying a perspiring three-hundred-pound trophy which she had been fortunate enough to capture.

"Yo' is de cook, is yo'?" the Wildcat said to the newly enthroned ruler of the kitchen.

The ebony Amazon looked at him. "Who is you?"

"I's champion ration battler ob de world. Wait till I gits back." The

Wildcat returned presently with an armful of wood. "You claims you's a cook--well, woman, I lights de fiah. Den you sees kin yo'."

"Kin I what?"

"Fust yo' barbecues 'at ham hangin' theh. When Ah gits th'oo, half of it will be lef'. Whilst de ham's sizzlin' you th'ows enough cawn bread togetheh to fill de big pan. When Ah gits th'oo dey'll be half of it lef'. When de ham juice begins to git sunburned you makes some ham gravy. Ah spec' ham gravy's de fondest thing Ah is of. I says 'Howdy, ham gravy!' an' afteh me an' de vittles gits acquainted, mah appetite won't need grub no mo'n a fish needs shoes."

"Cut de ham." The Wildcat carved off five or six thick slices.

The cook looked at him. "Is you fo'gittin' me?"

"You hungry? De way you looks, yo's et all de grub whut is."

"Nach'ral to be fat. Look at de elephant. How come you so skinny?"

"Wah mis'ry. All I et fo' two yeahs in France wuz Guv'ment rashuns. Dey wuzn't fillin'. I et myse'f down to boy-size pants de fust yeah. Secon' yeah dey lets me run wild 'cause dey couldn't find no unifawm small enough."

"Wuz yo' in de big drive?"

"I'll say I wuz. Us boys drove more railroad spikes at St. Sulpice dan a colonel has cooties. Woman, how come you knows all about de names ob de wah?"

"I had a husban' uplifteh in de wah whut wrote me letters. Mebbe yo' met up wid him, name bein' Huntington Boone."

The Wildcat's jaw sagged open as far as the roots of his lolling tongue. "Honey Tone! De uplifteh? He's yo' man?"

"You knows him?'

"Ah knows him some--goin' on a thousan' francs he lifted off me wid de gallopin' ivory."

"Ain't de same one. Huntington saw de light an' swerve f'm de sin road to de straight an' narrow in de Fall Revival five yeahs back--de time Sis Ellers got drowned at de baptisin' an' stayed undeh till she blowed up at Vicksbu'g. Mah man went oveh as a uplifteh."

"'At's de boy. He swerved back at de sinful life. De on'y upliftin' he done wuz wid us boys' money an' coonyak."

The Wildcat was thoughtful for a moment.

"Whah at is he now?" he suddenly asked.

"I ain't seed him since he went away. Wore out mah black alpaca mournin' dress an' spilt icecream all oveh de otheh at a social. 'At's how come Ah's in calico."

"I ain't seed him neveh since--"

"Since when?"

"Since he sailed fo' N' O'leans on de iron boat."

"He done come back! Praise de Lawd!"

"Call de police, you means. Did he git back he's in de jail whah at he belongs--all I seed wuz him leavin'."

In the face of the Wildcat's argument the Amazon's mood changed. "When I gets th'oo wid' dat man de jail folks sho' have to pen him up in a barrel to hol' de leavin's. He's 'bout as pop'lar wid me as smallpox. All he eveh done wuz bear down hahd on de money when I come home wid mah wages."

At the moment the Wildcat did not feel constrained to explain that Honey Tone's departure from Bordeaux had been one of the Wildcat's contrivings--one in which Honey Tone had been battened down in the hold of the cargo ship, together with a hundred French Colonial negro troops. "I rec'lects he lef' Bo'deaux on a boat dey calls de Princess Clam, headed fo' N' O'leans. Chances is he's in de N' O'leans jail right now."

The Wildcat decided that it might be well to encourage Honey Tone's mate to souse the black mood of her mourning in the whitewash of jealousy. "'Spect he might be married up again--mebbe. 'At boy gits 'gaged wheheveh 'at he goes."

"Is he rampagin' roun' I makes two widows stid of one does I ketch him. Cleah outen heah!"

Honey Tone's vindictive mate craved solitude in which to enjoy the misery of her ambition for revenge.

The Wildcat cleared out, taking with him a substantial segment of corn bread and two hot slices of ham. "Does Honey Tone live th'oo whut de female 'ception committee g'wine to git ready fo' him I gives him mah Craw de Gare an' all de woun' stripes whut is."

In the woodshed back of Captain Jack's house the mascot Lily patiently awaited her proprietor.

"Blaa!" she said in greeting when the Wildcat appeared.

"Whut yo' mean? How come you always craves nutriment?" the Wildcat demanded. "Heah." He gave the goat a fragment of corn bread. "Whuf! de ol' cawn pone sho' is fillin'. I sleeps me now fo' a little while. Den I goes downtown an' says Howdy to de boys. Lily, lay off dat hat! Eat de ham grease offen it does yo' crave to, but ca'm yo' se'f when yo' gits to de hat part."

The Wildcat reclined on a pile of hickory stove-wood and went to sleep. Sleeping was his long suit. At ten o'clock that night he woke up.

"Sho' is late. Front do' de barber shop be locked, but de back do' ain't." The Wildcat threaded the dark streets which led to Willie Webster's barber shop. The shave-and-haircut part of the Webster establishment served but to camouflage the darker industries which had their being in a room contiguous to the one where shaves were a nickel and haircuts fifteen cents, including musk.

At the back door of the barber shop the Wildcat hesitated for a moment in an effort to recall the secret knock which gained admittance in the days before the war. This element of the ritual finally came to him, and on the rough panels of the door sounded three quick raps followed by two at more deliberate intervals.

"I gits it 'fused up wid de time I wuz outeh guard to de Lodge ob Colored Damons. 'At knock wuz fo' an' th'ee. Fish club knock wuz two an' two. 'Membehs dat. Dat's how de animals come off de Ark, time ob de flood."

The door opened an inch, and the slot of light from within was interrupted by a rolling eyeball which surmounted a pair of questioning liver-coloured lips. "Who dat?"

"Wildcat--Vitus Marsden." The door opened quickly, and the Wildcat edged into the company of his former associates.

"Men, howdy!"

"Dogged if it ain't ol' Marsden! Boy, how is yo'? Is yo' back f'm de wah?"

"Heah us is, ain't I?"

Willie Webster, the proprietor of the establishment, came forward. "Don' see no arms an' no laigs missin'. Yo' neveh used yo' haid nohow, 'ceptin' to eat wid. Boy, how is yo'? Hail de Konk'rin' Hero!"

"Tol'able, Willie." The Konk'rin' Hero looked about him. At a table against the wall, under the rays of a smoking coal oil lamp, a crap game was in progress.

The Wildcat's fingers began to itch. He walked over toward the table. In the outline of one of the figures standing beside the table the Wildcat identified an acquaintance of his former days. "Seems like I knows de shape 'at boy's got." The Wildcat edged up to the table.

The owner of the familiar silhouette faced the Wildcat. "Wilecat, how is you? Hot dam, boy--is you back?"

Honey Tone Boone, the exile uplifter, was quick to conceal the inconvenient recognition in the extended palm of cordial insincerity.

The Wildcat's mouth opened and closed in cadence with the wild leaping of his Adam's apple. With difficulty he pacified his organs of speech, and presently the honey of hypocrisy filtered from the tip of his tongue. "Honey Tone! Honey Tone de uplifteh! Las' time I seed yo', yo' wuz in Bo'deaux."

"Las' time you seed me I wuz in trouble."

"How come?" A mask of surprise covered the Wildcat's face.

Honey Tone explained the method of his departure from Bordeaux.

"You kidnapped in de gizzard ob de ol' iron boat! Ain't it s'prisin'! Us boys sho' missed you."

Honey Tone relapsed into the vernacular. "I'll say 'at's all you missed. After you made de las' pass wid de gallopin' ivory you sho' lef me clean. All I had on me wuz cooties. How come you heah, Wilecat?"

"Cap'n Jack brung me. I's still workin' fo' Cap'n Jack. Afteh us landed offen de boat f'm France us rode de train clear across de country. Jes' broke loose f'm de army in time to keep f'm gittin' sent to Russia--place whah dey bury you. What you doin' heah?"

Honey Tone evaded a direct answer. "How's all de rest ob de boys?"

"Ain't seed 'em. Me an' Cap'n Jack came back casual."

"Whah at's he now?"

"Livin' heah. Memphis is de Cap'n's home town. Us jus' got in heah yes'day. F'm now on I works fo' Cap'n Jack. Ain't much to do, an'

Cap'n's lady sho' foun' a good cook. I aims to eat heavy f'm now on to
ketch up wid whut I missed in de army. Whut is you doin', 'sides
lookin' fo' easy money?"

Honey Tone, the ex-uplifter, was silent for a minute, and then his
organizing instinct welled strong.

"Me? I's organizin' a Returned Heroes' Parade. Us Konk'rin' Heroes what
wore de army unifawm jines in de gran' ruckus."

"Sho! Honey Tone, whut yo' mean army unifawm? You was 'fested with
letheh straps an' uppity talk when I knowed you fust. Now you talks
plain niggah."

"Sounds more homelike." Honey Tone did not feel constrained to explain
the finesse which prompted him to abandon the vocabulary which he had
derived from a year's schooling and considerable subsequent
speech-making.

"Aftah de parade mebbe us organizes de Colored Militarriers of America.
I's been ponderin' considerable how come some ob you ain't started dat
lodge yet? Dues a dollah a month. Parades fo' baptisn's, marryin's, and
funerals. Special buryin' department wheh you gits crematized or
secluded in de ground as you prefers, dependin' whether you pays fo'
bits a week extra or not."

"Sounds half gran'--mebbe folks takes up wid it. Ol' parade sho' sounds
noble." In common with other overseas veterans, the Wildcat listened
strong to the appeal made by the jingling hardware of heroism. He had
visions of himself prancin' along where white folks could look at
him--visions which included an O.D. uniform plentifully festooned with
wound stripes, coloured ribbons, service chevrons, and a few decorative
military crosses.

The group about the crap table thinned out. The Wildcat picked up the dice. "Does you crave high life, Honey Tone, read a chapteh f'm de clickers."

"I might ride a couple of r'ars," the uplifter conceded.

The Wildcat produced a bulky roll. Several pairs of gleaming eyeballs about him testified to the exceptional dimensions of his capital.

To the Wildcat's surprise Honey Tone hauled out a wallet in which lay a thick package of twenty-dollar bills. Hope burned strong in the Wildcat's chest, and with the flame of hope the Wildcat warmed the dice within his hand.

"Shoots ten dollahs. Fade me, Honey Tone, does you crave action."

"You's faded."

"Wham! Ah lets it lay. Shoots twenty dollahs."

"Roll 'em." Honey Tone dropped a twenty-dollar bill, which landed as gently as a snowflake on the green surface of the table. "Bam! Five an' a deuce."

Under the heat of the Wildcat's luck the uplifter's green snowflake melted into his opponent's roll.

"Ah lets it lay. Shoots fo'ty. Fo'ty ways. Shower down, Honey Tone. Mah luck builds homes fo' de ignorant poor. I's got de musk smell. Bam! Land, little Dove ob Peace. Land wid yo' bill full ob greens. An' I reads fo' tray!"

The Wildcat gathered in his winnings. He laid a twenty-dollar bill on the green table. "Fade me is you frantic."

Honey Tone covered the bet.

"Gallopers, pay de rent. Wham! Morning, rainbow. Wah just begun. Dove ob Peace got one hot end, like a hornet. Gallopers, see kin yo' uplift de Honey Tone Jack."

The dice raced on their victorious way.

Twenty minutes later Honey Tone Boone picked up the cubes. The capital in his leather pocket book had dwindled to a pair of weak-looking dollar bills. He reached into his pocket, and his hand came forth clutching a rubber-banded cylinder of currency whose external unit was a yellow obligation wherein the United States Government promised to pay the bearer fifty dollars in gold coin, providing the Democrats overlooked that much.

Honey Tone voiced his challenge.

"Shoots a hund'ed dollahs. De big coin keeps de pikers out."

The Wildcat batted his eyes, but rallied nobly and covered Honey Tone's bet with five twenties. "Roll 'em," he said huskily.

Honey Tone, rolling 'em, neglected to advertise the fact that when he reached for his new stake he had switched the dice.

"Seven. Shoots two hund'ed."

"Talk to 'em, Honey Tone." One of the uplifter's admirers offered verbal encouragement.

"Dey does de talkin'. Shower down, Wildcat. Shoots two hund'ed."

The Wildcat hesitated.

"Shower down," Honey Tone repeated. "You craves action. Git in de collar. Don't stan' theh poisoned on one foot, like de iron lady in de park."

The Wildcat glanced about him. He saw several pairs of heavy lips curling in the bow of derision. He counted out a handful of greenbacks. "'At's two hund'ed," he said heavily. "Roll 'em." His neck itched. He sensed the impact of the axe. "How come I crazy?"

The rolling dice halted. The class in addition announced that four and three made seven.

"I mows de lettuce." Honey Tone picked up his winnings. "Shoots a hund'ed."

The Wildcat audited his capital. "Sixty's all I got."

"Shoots sixty."

The Wildcat took a deep breath and held on to it until he read on the clicking cubes the final message of disaster.

"Whuf! 'At's me." Honey Tone looked at his victim, and in the glance of triumph glowed the dull fire of accomplished revenge.

"Dem bones says who is de Konk'rin' Hero. Dey knows."

The Wildcat picked up the dice and looked them over carefully. "Dice, wuz clothes a nickel I'se nekked--an' you done it."

Honey Tone reached for the dice. "How come?" he objected.

"Dese dice knows so much Ah thought mebbe dey's educated."

The uplifter was glad enough to ignore the remark in his effort to get the dice under cover. He switched the subject quickly to one which would not include an examination of his paraphernalia of chance. "I counts on you, Wilecat, to be colonel ob de parade."

"Me?" The Wildcat sobered under the responsibility.

"You be de walkin' colonel leadin' de Konk'rin' Heroes."

"Whah at does you come in?"

"I's de ridin' gin'ral whut leads."

"Honey Tone, does you ride, I does. You an' me is 'quivalent, only I's mo' in dis Konk'rin' Hero business. All de konk'rin' you eveh done wuz leadin' de sleep squad o' else joyin' roun' in Bo'deaux. No suh! Does you ride, I does."

"De ridin' part's de hardest. I rides so you boys kin see me give signs whah at to march. Does you ride, de nex' boy done crave to. He say, 'Whah at's mah mule?' Fust thing yo' knows, all de Konk'rin' Heroes would be on mules. Dey wouldn't be no more mules lef' in de world. Figgeh out what 'ud happen to de Horn Band when de mules heard de toots an' started tromplin' 'em down. Figgeh out could a band ride mules and play, bofe. Figgeh out some mo' wid yo' haid, 'stid of usin' it to eat wid so much, an' yo' might figgeh out I's right."

The logic in Honey Tone's objections appealed to the Wildcat. His imagination painted a contest between the Horn Department of the brunet brass band and three or four hundred stampeding mules. "I guess yo' says sense," he admitted. "Us boys walks."

For a little while he and Honey Tone discussed the details of the impending parade. "When us passes de' gran'stan'," the uplifter specified, "I gives de salute. You be leadin' de platoon. When you gits opposite de gran'stan' yo' says 'Eyes right.' 'At's all you does, 'ceptin' to keep marchin'."

"Who's gwine to be in de gran'stan'?"

"In de gran'stan'? Fust dere'll be de 'ception committee, den all religious organizations, den all de lodges an' grave clubs, den all de women an' chillen whut ain't 'filiated wid nothin' but husban's an' kitchen stoves."

Throughout the discussion the Wildcat's unmounted disappointment ached until it was suddenly quieted by a detail of the forthcoming ceremonies which he did not impart to his associate. In the Wildcat's brain was born a scheme which promised to balance the books between him and Honey Tone.

"Yo' wife be sittin' in de gran'stan', I s'pose?"

Honey Tone laid himself open to the serious fall which is the common sequel of deceit. "I ain't got no wife."

"Thought yo' tol' me you wuz a married man when Ah knowed you fust." The Wildcat was indulging in a little exploration.

"Did I say I wuz married I must've been crazy o' lyin'."

"You is both," the Wildcat inwardly reflected. "'At's at," he said to Honey Tone. "On'y, wid so much 'flooence, it 'pears like you'd furnish yo' own mule."

"Ain't I made yo' Supreem Gran' Arrangeh? You p'vides de mule. I takes care o' rentin' de' gran'stan' at de ball park an' spreadin' de publicity. Afterwards us has a gran' rally. Mebbe I makes a speech."

With the details of the program accomplished, the defeated Wildcat left the Konk'rin' Hero in the barber shop and made his way toward Captain Jack's home and the woodshed wherein was tethered the mascot goat.

Halfway up the alley which led to the woodshed the Wildcat spoke aloud in the darkness. "Konk'rin' Hero! Him ridin' de mule an' us boys ridin' ouah feet. Huh! I's de Supreem Gran' Walkin' Arrangeh, is I? Well, tomorrow I starts arrangin'." His monologue was suddenly interrupted by an explosive braying which burst from the woodshed adjoining the one in which rested Lily. The Wildcat surrendered to his racing legs and galloped a panic jazz to the exit of the alley before his common-sense reacted. "Sho! Me a Konk'rin' Hero!" He chuckled softly to himself. "Ol' mule whut b'longs to Cap'n Jack's neighbour sho' unkonkered me."

He retraced his steps until he came to the door of Captain Jack's woodshed. He opened the door and entered. From the darkness his mascot goat greeted him.

"Blaa!" said Lily.

"Ain't yo' asleep yit? Mebbe dat damn ol' mule woke you up. Git to sleep!" The Wildcat removed his shoes and lay down on a rickety bed in a corner of the woodshed. "I'll do the arrangin', Honey Tone," he mumbled. His lower jaw sagged, and into his open mouth whined a lone

mosquito. At the portals of sleep his night was again interrupted by
the mule in the adjoining shed.

"Dat's de night-brayin'est jug-head Ah eveh seed. Wuss'n a midnight
roosteh drunk wid moonlight." He was about to launch a few burning
curses from a vocabulary which the mule could saggitate, when a new
thought was born to him. He lay silent, staring above him into the
darkness.

"I's de Supreem Gran' Arrangeh!" he suddenly exclaimed. "I's de double
Grandes' Arrangeh whut is!" A faint bleat sounded from the darkness.
"Shut up, Lily! Fo' I gits th'oo arrangin', yo' an' me bofe rides de
mule does us crave to."

CHAPTER II

1.

The following morning the Wildcat gorged himself on a ponderous
breakfast. "Sho' is noble ham. Yo' sho' is de grandes' cook whut is.
Wondeh how come ol' Honey Tone neveh 'spressed himse'f about yo'?"

"'At niggah neveh wuz home enough to git 'quainted."

The Wildcat looked sidewise at the cook. "Last night I meets up wid a
boy in de barber shop whut knows Honey Tone pussonal. He says 'at
triflin' uplifteh claims to bein' single--claims he neveh had no wife."

The culinary Amazon picked up a frying pan and brought it down on the top of the range with a resounding bang. "He claims, does he? Wunst Ah gits mah hooks in 'at nigger's head, all he claims is funeral benefits!"

The Wildcat suggested that Honey Tone was probably far, far away and established as the centre of another family circle. The cook reacted nobly.

He waited until the avoirdupois cyclone had cooled off. Something in the cook's energetic rage suggested the activities of the Wildcat's former landlady, Cuspidora Lee, from whom he had occasionally borrowed tobacco money. He determined to visit his former boarding house and renew his financial relations.

"You has my sympathy bofe ways," he said to the cook. "Yo' is married up wid a no-account triflin' yellow uplifteh. Is he wid you, you is mis'able, an' is he A.W.O.L. yo' is twice 'at much. Wuz I you, when you meets up wid him I'd bleed him by han'. But don' you grieve. Neveh min'. Some day yo' meets up wid him…. Den yo' pays him back."

2.

The Wildcat left the kitchen. He carried a bouquet of cabbage leaves to Lily, who was tethered at the woodshed door. "Eat heavy, Lily," he commanded. "Yo' neveh got no reliable greens like dis when yo' wuz in France." He hazed Lily into the woodshed and departed on his way to visit Miss Cuspidora Lee. He found the Lee personage perspiring darkly in the clouds of heat that billowed from a red-hot cookstove.

"Cuspido', I bids yo' mawin'," he said briefly.

Cuspidora Lee turned upon him. "Fo' de Lawd sake, you scared me! If it ain't Vitus Marsden. Prodigal, come heah! Whah at is you been?" The Wildcat was engulfed in an embrace which reminded him of the time he had been buried under seven tons of fermented hay.

He came to the surface. "Cuspido', sho' is glad to see you. Whah at's dem pussonal preserves you 'scribed 'bout in yo' letteh?"

"Sit down till I feeds yo'. Is you as hungry as you always wuz I reckon you massacrees all de vittles in de house."

After the Wildcat had eaten within an inch of his life he sat back from the table and took a deep breath. "Whuf! Stomach's gittin' so big mah arms won' reach pas' it. Does it keep on mebbe Ah's 'bliged to turn roun' an' eat backwa'ds. Sho' is noble rashuns. Noblest rashuns I eveh et wuz heah."

He consumed an hour recounting his adventures in France for the benefit of Cuspidora Lee. At the conclusion of the recital the Wildcat was invited to make his abode in the Lee residence.

"Craves to, Cuspido', but Ah kain't. Ol' Cap'n Jack needs me. Wunst I leaves ol' Cap'n, dat boy run wild an' Ah finds him out in San F'mcisco. Ah'll be draggin' 'long now. Sees yo' in de gran'stan' at de ball park during de Konk'rin' Heroes' Parade nex' Thursday."

"You sees me befo' dat. I's givin' a weegee pa'ty We'n'sday night, an' I bids yo' welcome."

"How come weegee?"

"Ain't you know weegee--little boa'd whut points out is you or ain't you an' how come in de pas', present, an' future?"

"Sho! How de boa'd know?"

"Spirits. Man whut sells de boa'ds runs de spirits."

"Is you tryin' to plague me?"

"You come heah Wensday night an' see is I."

The Wildcat returned to Captain Jack's residence. "Sho' is gran' to git home," he reflected. "Parades, weegee pa'ties--fust thing Ah knows Ah'll be claimed by de church sociables. Sho' beats France. Stays heah an' works fo' ol' Cap'n Jack, eats me heavy, raises Lily, 'filiates at de barber shop wid de boys. Sho' beats de A.E.F. wah bizness."

His daydreaming was interrupted by Captain Jack's commanding voice.

"Wildcat, come here."

"Cap'n, yessuh."

"I'm going away for three months," Captain Jack abruptly announced. Then he added: "Keep your eye on things."

"Cap'n, yessuh. Goin' 'way!... When does us staht?"

"Us don't start. For once in my life I hope to go some place and come back without being hounded by my Wildcat nigger."

"Cap'n, yessuh. Whut beats me is how yo' aims to git along widout me takin' keer o' you. You neveh wuz no single thriveh."

"I'll get along without you. Go in and lock up the trunks."

"Mis' Cap'n Jack gwine wid you?"

"I'll say she is. Whither I goeth there shall she also go. Git those trunks fixed up."

With the departure of the master of the house a cloud of melancholy settled about the Wildcat which was not dispelled until suppertime.

3.

On Wednesday night the Wildcat soused himself with bay rum and musk. About his neck, in lieu of a collar, he wrapped the spliced sleeves of a discarded silk shirt whose cerise dyes had barred it from Captain Jack's wardrobe. On his feet he wore a pair of patent leather violins whose tight interiors had been plentifully massaged with axle grease.

He started out with his mascot. "C'm on heah, Lily--you stahts gittin' social wid quality folks. How come dese shoes pinches all de time sho' beats me. By rights I weahs twelves. Man whut sold dese shoes said dey wuz fifteens--feels like sho' take bofe to make 'at much. But when dey sees dis heah neckerchief dey won't notice de shoes."

Halfway to the weegee party he removed the shoes and carried them in his hand to the portals of the Lee establishment. He sat down outside the door of the ouija castle and put on his shoes. He tethered Lily at the step and knocked at the door. A moment later he was being greeted by twenty friends and half as many strangers.

"Befo' I turns down de lights," the hostess announced, "I wants you to meet up wid Colonel Boone, one ob de culled heroes whut made de wah safe fo' white folks. Colonel Boone, say howdy at Misteh Marsden."

The Wildcat and the uplifter again stood face to face. "Honey Tone, how come Cuspido' calls you 'Colonel'?"

"By rights 'at's mah rank."

"By rights you is rank." The Wildcat turned to his brunette hostess. "Ah knows dis Boone man. Met up wid him in France. How come he projectin' roun' heah?"

Cuspidora was quick to sense a rift of jealousy in the social lute. "He's aimin' to claim me fo' a weddin' mate."

She made haste to switch the deal.

"Blow out dat light, Sis' Mosby." She reached for a second coal oil lamp and turned it down until the room was hardly light enough to distinguish the black letters on the ouija board which lay on the table. The uplifter deflected the impending embarrassment which might develop from continued conversation with the Wildcat by functioning as master of ceremonies.

"Rally roun'. Spirits is willin' if de flesh ain't weak. Wilecat, fondle de weegee board an' take a ra'r at seein' whut de future holds."

"How come?"

"Dis corner says, 'Yes.' Dat corner says, 'No.' De little board slides Yes or No, dependin' how de spirits answers whut yo' asks."

The cross-examination of Mr. Ouija and his talented aggregation of spirits endured for an hour, during which time a number of interesting facts concerning various members of the assemblage became public property.

The Wildcat, returning from an enjoyed battle at the refreshment corner of Cuspidora Lee's parlor, wedged his way into the group about the ouija board and laid a heavy hand thereon. The memory of Cuspidora's statement concerning her love affair with Honey Tone rankled within him.

"Spirits," he said, "I axes yo' is I married?"

Ouija answered, "No."

"Is Honey Tone Boone married?"

The board became a battlefield. Presently the tight tendons of the uplifter's hand showed grey against his skin, but without avail, because the Wildcat's little finger lay tight against the perimeter of the moving planchette. Impelled by the Wildcat's little finger the implacable spirits hazed Weegee to the "Yes" corner of the board.

Honey Tone's defeated fingers relaxed. "Dat's de lyin'est board I eveh see. How come yo' gits a lyin' weegee board, Mis' Lee?"

"Spirits neveh lies." The hostess defended her unseen assistants.

"Ain't no lyin' lef' to do afteh dese upliftehs gits th'oo," the Wildcat commented.

A little later, apart from the other guests, the Wildcat asked Cuspidora Lee a direct question. "O! Honey Tone been representin' he's single?"

The Wildcat's brunette hostess hesitated. "Tol' me he neveh seed nobody befo'," she admitted--"tol' me his love-eye neveh seed nobody 'ceptin' me."

"All 'at boy's love-eye seed is de p'visions in yo' kitchen. Ah knows him. Acts like de yelleh niggah whut he is--prancin' round uppity in France--comes back heah callin' himself 'Colonel,' 'count he wore oilcloth leggin's an' drunk coonyak whilst us boys wuz fightin' de battle of Bo'deaux."

Cuspidora Lee listened with eager ears. "I runs him out now, the flea-bit houn'," she finally announced.

"Ca'm yo'se'f. Don' git to brindlin'. Come out to de ball park tomorr' at de parade an' you sees him leadin' us Culled Heroes."

Honey Tone Boone meanwhile had charmed a dozen of his male and female auditors with Mister Ouija's spiritual assistance.

At eleven o'clock the coal oil lamps were again lighted and the guests employed themselves in the pleasurable business of consuming such refreshments as the Wildcat had overlooked. The evening ended with a general announcement from the uplifter, in which he invited the assemblage to be present on the following day at the parade of the Konk'rin' Culled Heroes.

"As de Supreem Gran' Organizeh Ah bids yo' welcome," he concluded.

From the darkness outside came a sardonic echo. "Blaa!" Lily the mascot had seen fit to accept the uplifter's invitation.

When the party broke up, the uplifter showed an inclination to linger after the Wildcat made his departure, but presently he realized the failure of his ambition.

"Come on heah, Honey Tone," the Wildcat invited. "I walks a ways wid yo'."

Once along the dark street Honey Tone sought to review the ouija performance. "What fo' wuz you shovin' weegee an' makin' de spirits say 'yes' when they craved to say 'no'?"

"How come shovin'? Spirits does de shovin'. Ol' weegee tells de truf'. Yo' sho' is married, ain't yo'?"

"I tells you once I ain't. I tells you now I ain't, Don' say no mo'."

"When you talks 'at way you sho' sounds lak a Cunnel, Honey Tone."

The Wildcat switched the conversation to the details of the parade.

"Is all de 'rangements done?"

"'Rangements done, 'ceptin' de mule I rides."

"Ah'll git de mule. Whah at does I meet you?"

"Parade stahts at noon f'm Willie Webster's barbeh shop. Us marches th'oo town an' hol's de gran' review at de ball park."

A little farther down the street the two halted. "Whah at does you live, Honey Tone?" the Wildcat inquired.

Honey Tone did not see fit to reveal the location of his present domicile. "Down de street a ways," he said.

The pair parted. "Don' fo'git mah parade-leadin' mule fo' tomorrow," Honey Tone admonished, "an' 'blige me by not referrin' no mo' to no wife whut I ain't got."

"Ah'll 'blige him," the Wildcat mentally conceded. "Afteh tomorrow Ah don't need to do no wife-referrin' 'bout Honey Tone."

The Wildcat went to sleep that night enjoying the details of a plan wherein Honey Tone's radiant future was considerably overcast by the clouds of retribution.

CHAPTER III

1.

At breakfast on the following morning he repeated his invitation to Captain Jack's cook. "Ol' Cap'n an' de Lady bofe gone away. No need you stayin' roun' here all de time. Git to de gran'stan' early an' git a front seat. Mebbe you'll meet up wid one ob mah pussonal lady fren's--Cuspidora Lee, whut I boa'ded wid befo' de wah claimed me. Cuspido' said she g'wine to weah a big pink hat wid yaller feathers. 'At's how you knows her. You sees me an' mah mascot when us swings pas' de gran' stan'. Ah'll be follerin' de Supreem Leader. He be ridin' a mule."

The Wildcat spent the next half hour festooning his mascot goat with raiment appropriate for the grand march. Lily's O.D. service coat was brightened with a red tissue paper sash. The Wildcat sewed a turkey wing fan to the mascot's overseas cap and wired the gaudy combination securely in place between Lily's horns.

"Hot dam! I says you parades." For himself he borrowed a few things which lay here and there in the trunk room of Captain Jack's house. He stowed his own paraphernalia in a gunnysack. Leading Lily, he made his way to the neighbour's woodshed wherein was stabled the overgrown night-braying mule.

"Gimme dis heah mule, boy--an' a saddle," he said to the brunet guardian of the neighbour's mule. "I needs him temporary."

"How come?"

"I craves him fo' de Culled Heroes' Parade. Some day I gives you two bits does you lend him half a day. All he does in heah is eat you po' an' wake folks up."

"Whah at's de two bits?" The exchange was effected, and presently, leading the mule and the festooned mascot, the Wildcat arrived at the rendezvous in front of Willie Webster's establishment. He tethered the mule to a hitching post and led Lily into the barber shop.

"How come de goat?" one of the assemblage questioned.

"See dem stripes? Lily went th'oo more battles dan you has sense. F'm now on, whah at I is, Lily is. Bible says, 'Whah at de goat, dere is Ah also goat.' Stan' up heah, Lily."

The mascot was vainly endeavouring to eat the feathers from the top of her own head.

"Ca'm yo'se'f. Whah at's de Supreem Parade Leadeh?"

Honey Tone Boone stepped out of the adjoining room. "'At you, Wildcat? Whah at's mah steed?"

"Hitched outdoors. Sho' is rarin' to go. Parade-leadinest mule Ah eveh see."

Honey Tone took a look through the window at his conspicuous mount. "Sure looms up. How come de goat?"

"'At goat's mah pussonal luck."

Honey Tone looked sideways at the Wildcat. "Does yo' feel like backin' yo' luck wid a jingle, mebbe I 'bliges yo' sudden. Dey's a racetrack in de back room does you crave to gallop yo' luck a couple of heats."

The Wildcat accepted the challenge. The pair walked quickly into the back room.

"Shoots a dollah!" He explored himself for silver and revised his challenge. "Shoots fifty cents. Ain't got but sixty, an' I needs a dime fo' goobers does I lose."

"Boy, roll 'em." Honey Tone proffered a pair of anxious dice, but the Wildcat paid no attention to the offer.

"I got mah pussonal weapons," he said. He fished a pair of dice from his left shoe. "Dey speaks de language. Gallopehs, git right. Wham! Ah tol' you! Ah lets it lay. Shoots a dollah."

Honey Tone faded the bet. "Roll 'em." The Wildcat touched the tips of his fingers to Lily's head. "Goat, stan' by me." His swinging hand released a pair of dice whose innocent upturned faces presently revealed a four and a trey. "Seven! Ah lets it lay. Whole hog o' de squeal."

"Roll 'em!"

"Bam. Six an' five. Ah done climbed de luck tree. Honey Tone, shake me out. Shoots fo' dollahs. Lily, stan' by me!"

"Blaa!" remarked Lily.

"Boy, roll 'em." Honey Tone began to itch for possession of the dice.

"Asleep in de snowdrift. When Lily says 'blaa' Ah lets 'em ride."

"An' seven! Ah lets it lay."

"Shoot, you fool, nobody neveh made five passes."

"Nobody but me." The Wildcat opened his dusky palm and a natural seven leaped to the gaze of a waiting world. Honey Tone's eyes bulged with surprise.

The Wildcat accumulated his winnings. From the crumpled handful of bills he selected a dollar bill, which he twisted into a tempting little salad bouquet. "Lily, eat this fo' luck. Ah reaps de greens to nutrify mah mascot! Shoots ten dollahs!"

Lily munched delicately on the dollar bill while the Wildcat continued with the harvest. The deeper Honey Tone sank into the bogs of chance, the more he resented the introduction of the Wildcat's trained dice. Once, in the run of hard luck, he showed signs of weakening, but the Wildcat was quick to rally him with the adroit tongue of flattery.

"One thing I'll say fo' Honey Tone--win or lose, dat boy rides along. Sho' is a vet'ran sport."

In the Wildcat's compliment Honey Tone's effort to unload from the wreckbound train of chance found defeat. He rode along, hope springing eternal, until his financial condition approximated zero.

"Shoots twenty dollars." The Wildcat's announcement leaped from a pair of belligerent lungs.

"Ain't got but 'leven fifty." Honey Tone's voice was husky.

"Shoots 'leven fifty." The game was delayed a moment while the Wildcat hunted for appropriate minor currency. "Heah's de fifty cents I stahted wid. Lily, at ease!" The Southern Hemisphere of the mascot subsided.

"Honey Tone, you sin-'fested uplifteh, feel de axe. Bam! Dey reads four trey. Lily, at res'."

The victorious Wildcat added the last of his winnings to the bulky roll inside his pocket. "'At winds yo' up, big boy. De Supreem leadin' mule rides easier now. Yo' weighs six hund'ed dollahs less."

A unit on the outer fringe of the pop-eyed audience pressed forward to where the Wildcat stood. "Same ol' cyclone," he said in greeting. "Wilecat, you 'membehs me? I ain't seed sich a fust-class cleanin' since us fit de battle of Bo'deaux an' yo' win all de payday us boys got."

The Wildcat suddenly recognized the speaker. "Backslid! How come yo' heah? Hot dog! I sho' is glad to see yo'."

"Ah come home casual, count of stummik mis'ry th'ee weeks afteh yo' lef Bo'deaux," the Backslid Baptist explained. "Sho' is glad to see yo'."

"You 'membehs Honey Tone?" The Wildcat introduced the uplifter. "Honey

Tone leads de parade. Us starts in five minutes. Jine in, Backslid, an' yo' marches 'longside ob me an' Lily."

"Sho' 'steem to, Wilecat, but I takes mah run dis aftehnoon."

"How come run?"

"I's back on de ol' job runnin' Pullman out of Chicago. I's due out on de Fliah fo' Chicago at two-fo'ty. Any time yo' craves a ramble on de cushions, roun' me up. Ah stakes yo' to a white coat an' yo' is aced in as mah helpeh. Pullman service is crammed wid dead-head helpehs now de Guv'ment's runnin' de lines. An' Boy--once us 'rives at Chicago de gran' ruckus begins!"

"Backslid, 'at sho' sounds noble. Some day me an' Lily sho' make a trip wid you."

The Wildcat and his former associate were interrupted by Honey Tone Boone. "Wilecat, you's de Supreem Arrangeh, ain't you? Roun' up de humans. Fawm de parade. Us starts."

The Wildcat threw back his head and addressed the gathering in the barber shop. "Company, 'tenshun! All de niggahs in de room whut's gwine to jine de gran' parade, fall out de do' an' fall in!" He led the rush for the exit. Outdoors he repeated the announcement. "Gran' parade led by Honey Tone Boone. Followin' me an' Lily comes de brass ban'. Den comes de Sons ob Damon. Sons ob Damon wearin' de yellah belly ban's walks ahead. Followin' de Sons ob Damon, de Knights wid de Red Pants falls in. Parade marches fo' an' fo', ladies outside. Keep off de car tracks. Followin' de Knights wid de Red Pants comes de 'Filiated Toilers.

"Cornet Club comes nex', 'ceptin' de big bass drum. Fetch dat bass drum oveh heah. Yo' marches by me."

He turned to a group of human beings whose sole common characteristic was their colour and the colour of the sashes which were tied about them. "Whut outfit is you boys?"

"Us is de Committee ob Culled Democrats."

"How come they let you out ob jail? Fall in behin' de lunch wagon. 'At's whah you gin'lly is."

The drum-bamming giant took his place opposite the Wildcat. The Wildcat turned to the Supreme Organizer of the Culled Militarriers of America. "Git abo'ad 'at steed, Honey Tone," he said.

Honey Tone clambered on to the mule with the assistance of a pair of agile bystanders. The Wildcat closed his eyes and lifted his head high in the air. "Company, 'tenshun!" He turned to the drum-bammer opposite him. "Le-e-t's go!"

"Bam!" The crash inside the bass drum found a deafening echo in a blare of exploding horns and cornets. Lily shied close beside her master. Honey Tone's mule drooped a languid ear over a bulging eyeball as if to shut out a vision of impending disaster, and then, at the second note from the bass drum, the mule leaped into a wild gallop. Before the marchers had covered a hundred feet Honey Tone and his jug-head mount had passed the fire hall three blocks down the street.

The parade marched steadily toward the ball park. Ten minutes later Honey Tone and the mule clattered past the parade. "Ol' mule sho' steers noble, but he kain't stop," the Wildcat announced to the drum-bammer opposite him.

On Honey Tone's third visit the Wildcat called loudly to him. "Head 'at mule roun' nex' time an' back him in de ball park." The Supreme Organizer's reply was lost in a clatter of hoofs.

2.

At the ball park the parade waited for the intermittent uplifter. As Honey Tone galloped past the head of the column he did a Brodie and landed breathless against the big bass drum. "Boom!"

"Whuf!" he said. "Ketch dat mule!" The hero blood pulsed strong in the veins of the Knights with the Red Pants. They rallied to the rescue. The organization deployed, and presently the big night-braying mule was again delivered into Honey Tone's reluctant hands.

"Wait till Ah 'ranges 'at steed." The Wildcat loosened the saddle girth. Unseen by Honey Tone, he removed a small horseshoe from between the saddle blanket and the mule's epidermis. "Sho' brings de luck. Some boy got de luck hunch figgered wrong. Git aboa'd, Honey Tone.--Blanket got wrinkled. He done ca'm down now. Ah knows him. Git aboa'd an' lead de parade into de ball park an' pas' de gran'stan'."

In the face of the assemblage Honey Tone could not back down. He mounted the mule. To his surprise the animal walked slowly and with all the peculiar dignity that a mule can summon. The uplifter looked down at the Wildcat. "Line 'em up fo' de gran' entry," he said.

The Wildcat turned and called loudly to the marching column. "Company, 'tenshun! Heads up fo' de gran' entry." He turned to his companion. "Keep de drum goin'. Ah waits to see de parade git by an' is eve'ything arranged right." The Wildcat faded out. When the end of the marching column passed him he walked quickly to a policeman who was standing near the portals of the entrance to the ball park.

"Cap'n, suh," he said to the policeman, "'at mule leadin' de parade b'longs to Misteh Joe Carroll, whut's de neighbour ob Cap'n Jack Stuart, whah at I wucks. Ah ain't sayin' 'at ridin' niggah stole 'at mule, but Ah knows Misteh Carroll neveh lent him. 'At niggah's no good. Ah knows him."

"What outfit is this parade?" the officer asked.

"Ain't no outfit. 'At triflin' niggah on de mule claims he's organizin' a new lodge--gits folks wild to jine, and den lif's de 'nitiation money. Nex' day mebbe turns up in Vicksburg o' some place else whah some mo' fool niggahs craves to jine on wid him. He sho' don' b'long here. Ah knows him!"

A record is a record. An arrest is an arrest, and the capture of a mule thief is a star of magnitude in any one's official crown. The policeman walked into the ball park and headed across to where a companion officer was standing in front of the grandstand. At the moment, in the grandstand Cuspidora Lee and Captain Jack's cook, seated together, were just beginning to get acquainted. "Seems like I knows dat boy," the cook remarked. "'At boy on de big mule."

"I knows him too." The tenor of pride rang in Cuspidora's pronouncement. "Ah knows him well. He's de Supreem Parade Organizeh. 'At man's rich--on'y las' night at de weegee 'semblage in mah house he showed me nearly six hunn'ed dollahs. When de social visitin' part starts afteh de parade I gives yo' a howdy-do, does yo' crave to meet up wid him; but don' git triflin' wid him, woman. 'At's all. He's mah man."

"How come?"

Cuspidora brindled engagingly.

"Us aims to git married soon as de local organizin' is finished."

"Ain't it gran'? Whut yo' say his name is?"

Honey Tone and his trailing parade were plodding along toward Cuspidora Lee and Captain Jack's cook. When Honey Tone came closer Cuspidora waved archly at the Supreme Organizer.

"Whut yo' say his name is?" The ponderous cook at Cuspidora's side repeated her question.

The Lee lips answered absently. "Boone--Huntington Boone."

The cook swept the back of her hand across her eyes. "Boone! 'At's him!" She turned to Cuspidora. "You aims to marry him, does you? Well, marry him sudden. Ah aims to kill him. 'At niggah an' me married each other two yeahs befo' he went to wah!"

The cook bellowed hoarsely once in the Supreme Organizer's direction. "Honey Tone!" A shrill echo came from Cuspidora's lips. The Supreme Organizer wilted from the deck of his mule. Without looking around, he started for the entrance of the ball park, but before he had covered half the distance he was overtaken by a furious tigress. Cuspidora Lee had outdistanced Honey Tone's wife in her pursuit of the Organizer, and to her went first blood. At Cuspidora Lee's hands Honey Tone took the count just in time to get his chattering teeth full of his enraged wife's crunching heels. "Stan' back, Cuspido'! Ah aims to tromple 'at snake in de dust!"

Thereafter, for a space of minutes the massacre proceeded with systematic fury. It ended only when the policeman unlimbered a wicked sap and forcibly dragged the battling brunettes from their crumpled victim.

"Git to hell away from that nigger," the officer yelled at the two women. With the assistance of a hearty boost from the policeman, the Supreme Organizer struggled to his feet.

"Lemme go--lemme go!" he gasped.

Wham! The two-foot swagger stick in the hand of the police officer found its target. "Shut up, you mule-stealin' baboon. Come on here! You git fifty years in jail if we don't lynch you!"

Honey Tone Boone, the uplifter, trailed along with the policeman.

The Wildcat, with his mascot goat close beside him in the shadows of the entrance to the ball park, witnessed the consummation of his plans. "Ah'll say I's de Supreem Gran' Arrangeh!" he exulted. "Grandes' 'rangeh whut is! Eve'ything sho' is 'ranged noble."

He tied a leading-string around the mascot's neck. "Come on heah, Lily. Us fades befo' Honey Tone busts loose f'm de jail. Us rides de Fliah to Chicago wid ol'Backslid. He's mah fren'. Le's go!"

CHAPTER IV

"Memphis, let me miss you! Feet, see kin you trod de good-bye jazz! Lily, le's go! Git in step! C'm on heah befo' Ah jerks yo' head loose

I'm yo' horns."

Lily lagged. No guilty conscience impelled the mascot goat. In addition to this, lacking mental momentum, her progress was considerably impeded by a parade uniform consisting of an O.D. army shirt which dangled loosely about her forelegs.

Half a block down the street Lily's parade raiment slipped. Her hobbles tripped her. The galloping Wildcat felt an added drag on the leading string. He glanced backward in his flight.

"Goat, how come you lose the cadence? Doggone you, see kin you skid till you gits in step."

Lily bought the next fifty yards with an expenditure of some epidermis and two ounces of goat hair.

She regained her feet, staggering under a ponderous ambition for revenge. Forty feet from the Calhoun Street curb she took careful aim at the Wildcat and stepped on the accelerator. The Wildcat coasted into Calhoun Street with his parade-leading Prince Albert flapping straight out behind him. He skidded over the curb in a pose which cost his army pants half of their seating capacity.

Inertia claimed him. He rolled his head slowly over his shoulder and gazed in bewilderment upon his prancing Nemesis.

"Lily, at ease!" The goat ambled up beside him. "At res'!"

The Wildcat grabbed for the mascot's leading string. "You an' me declares peace. Ah done wrong when Ah drug you, but now see kin you ramble. Ah craves to reach de Chicago Fliah whah at de ol' Backslid Baptis' is porter, so us kin leave town without leadin' no mob."

"Blaa!" Lily answered in forgiveness.

About the mascot's chest the Wildcat adjusted the O.D. shirt with its
three service stripes. He tilted the little overseas cap which Lily
wore to a rakish angle between the mascot's horns.

With Lily clicking along at the Wildcat's heels, the pair entered the
portals of the Grand Central Station.

The Wildcat accosted a Red Cap of his own colour. "Whah at kin I find
de Backslid Baptist whut takes care o' de white gen'men on de Chicago
Fliah 'at leaves at 2:40?"

"I knows 'at boy dey calls Backslid, but dey ain't no Fliah leavin' at
2:40. 'At boy runs Pullman on de Panama Limited, leavin' heah at 10:10
tonight. Ol' Backslid neveh shows up till half-past nine to take his
cah out."

Confronted by seven intervening hours of life in Memphis, which might
include the release of Honey Tone Boone, whose temporary confinement in
the jail had just been accomplished, the Wildcat's ambition flopped.
His sole desire for the moment was for a high-grade segment of
camouflage or the sanctuary of a close-fitting black cave.

"Whah at kin me an' Lily hide out till mah fren' Backslid shows up?"

The Red Cap looked at him. "What you done--outrun a bullet f'm some
white man's gun, o' mebbe busted jail?"

The Wildcat's skin shrank a size or two at the mention of jail. "I
ain't done nuthin'. Fo'git dem jail words. All I got is business in
Chicago, an' I aims to ride wid de Baptist."

The Red Cap came to realize that the Wildcat sought to avoid publicity. "I knows a place whah you kin crawl undah a five-dollah bill an' hide."

"Whah at's de place?"

"Whah at's de five-dollah bill?"

The Wildcat produced the greenback. The Red Cap took it.

"C'm on heah wid me." He led the Wildcat and Lily to the rooms where Red Caps shifted from their civilian raiment to the uniform of their calling.

"Nobody but us boys neveh comes heah. Ah'll pass de word to de Backslid Baptis' to hunt you up when he 'rives f'm uptown tonight."

Until nine o'clock that night the Wildcat and Lily lay under cover. Shortly after nine o'clock the Backslid Baptist arrived at the station to board his Pullman, which would be cut into the Panama Limited.

He encountered the Wildcat in the latter's retreat.

"How come? When Ah seed you dis aftehnoon you an' Lily wuz in de parade-leadin' business, followin' Honey Tone Boone on de mule."

"Us changed since den, Backslid. Ol' Honey Tone done unconsecrate hisself f'm de parade-leadin' mule."

"Whah at is he now?"

"Safe in jail, whah at Cuspido' Lee an' de otheh wild woman kain't claim de remains. Whut time does us leave?"

"How come de 'us'?"

"I craves to furlough mahself loose f'm Memphis fo' a while. Does ol' Honey Tone git free mebbe he uprises agin' me."

"C'm on.... Us is due out at 10:10."

Before the Backslid Baptist was into his uniform a boy brought an order slip to him. He read it and handed it to the Wildcat.

The Wildcat looked at the paper.

"You knows Ah kain't read, Backslid. What 'at paper say?"

"Ah switches to a N'O'leans cah--de Mazeppa. Otheh boy's sick."

"How come he sick?"

"Some boys gits sick so as to miss Ol' Man Trouble. Might have made a cleanin' wid de bones. Might crave to meet up wid some fren's in Memphis. Kain't say how come. Us finishes de boy's run. Come on!"

The Backslid Baptist led the way to the platform in the long train shed. "Don't know kin I deadhead 'at goat."

"Sho' kin, Baptist. 'At mascot don't take up no room. 'At goat traveled f'm N'Yawk to San F'mcisco in de vegetable bin on a dinin' cah. Lily ain't no rampager."

When the Panama Limited roared into the train shed Lily cringed against the Wildcat's legs. "Stan' up theh! How come you scared at de ol' train?"

Followed by the Wildcat and Lily, the Backslid Baptist sought his car. "Whah at's de Mazeppa?" he asked the first porter whom he encountered.

"Hello, Backslid. Is you runnin' Mazeppa?"

"Aims to."

"Menagerie cah."

"How come?"

"Dogdest cahload ob folks Ah evah see. Wait till mawnin' an' you sees yo' passengers. 'At's de ol' battleship, five cahs back."

The Wildcat and Lily, in the wake of the Backslid Baptist, presently boarded the Mazeppa.

Once inside the car, the porter sniffed heavily. "Gin trip. Thank de Lawd ain't no kids. Don't smell no bananas. Lis'sen. Heah dat boy snore?"

"Snores lak he's chokin' to death."

"Ain't chokin'. 'At's a fat boy wid de alcohol snorts."

The Backslid Baptist sniffed again. "Sho' is."

"Is what?"

"Chorus girl lady, o' mebbe one ob dem movin' picture ladies."

"Ah'll say you does."

"Does what?"

"Sees an' heahs wid yo' nose. Did anybody bust you in de beak dey'd knock you deaf an' blind."

"Wilecat, Ah run Pullman ten yeahs--boy sho' gits deprived ob a lot ob ignorance in dat time. Sho' gits so he knows de folks on his cah quick. Gits to be a reg'lah mind readeh."

The Wildcat looked at the Backslid Baptist. "Whut dat fat boy wid de alcohol snorts thinkin' about?"

The mind-reading porter looked at the Wildcat. A slow smile cut a red gash in his face.

"Same as you--de half bottle whut's left."

"Ah'll say you's a mind reader. Read an' see does de half bottle need a guardeen."

"Fo'get dat guardeen business. Tomorrow mawin' he gives it to you does you crave it. 'At boy wouldn't look cross-eyed at you in town, but when you weahs de unifawm mos' likely does you crave a dram o' his liquor he be proud to give it to you. When him an' de headache wakes up tomorrow--"

Zing! From above the Wildcat's head an electric bell rang with the suddenness of a striking rattlesnake.

"Whut dat?"

"Ca'm yo'sef. Some passengeh ringin' fo' de porteh. Store dat goat in heah befo' de ol' train conductor comes th'oo."

The Backslid Baptist opened the door of the linen closet. Lily the mascot was ushered into the dark cave beneath the shelves.

"Lily, at res'! See kin you sleep whilst Ah learns de porter business." The Wildcat began to absorb the free ice-water.

Zing! The annunciator rang again with an impatient note.

"Put dis white coat on you whilst I sees who wants whut." The Backslid Baptist handed the Wildcat a white linen coat. The Wildcat removed his long parade-leading Prince Albert with the red plush sash and the yellow epaulets and donned the white jacket.

The Backslid Baptist returned from the far end of the car. "Fat boy in Loweh 7 wid de alcohol snorts craves ice-wateh. Fill a papeh cup an' carry it back to him."

The Wildcat filled a paper cup with ice-water and started down the aisle of the car. He returned presently.

"Kain't find whah at is 'at boy."

"You looks till you sees '7' on de curtains. 'At's whah he is."

The Wildcat essayed a second attempt with his life-saving ice-water. He had proceeded half the length of the car when, above the muffled rattles and creaks of its fabric, there lifted a wild shrieking laughter.

The paper cup in the Wildcat's clutching hand was crushed flat. From the cup there gushed a geyser of ice-water straight for the parted curtains of Lower 7.

CHAPTER V

The wild laughter from somewhere across the aisle continued, but now it was punctuated by three voices.

"F'r Gawd's sake, dearie, be quiet!"

"Spluff! What th' hell--"

"Lady Luck, whah at is you?"

The Wildcat galloped back along the swaying aisle to the protection of the Backslid Baptist.

The high-pitched laughter pursued him.

"Pull de stoppin' string, Baptis'! Ah craves to git off dis train."

"Ca'm yo'se'f. Whut ails you?"

"Heah dat laffin'? Heah dat crazy--"

Zing! Zing! ZING!

"Doggone 'at Loweh 7. Did you wateh dat boy?"

The Wildcat looked at the crushed cup in his hand. "Ah'll say so.

Missed 'at boy's neck, but de ol' ice-wateh sho' baptized him.'"

"See whut he wants again."

"You betteh see, Baptis'. I's just learnin'.'"

"Dearie, be quiet before I wring your neck!" A strident feminine voice addressed the author of the laughter. "Shut up! There, there, dearie.... Oh, you feen, leggo! My gawd, he bit me!"

"Purty purty burd. Purty purty burd."

"You feen!"

"Quawk!"

Down the length of the car, from between the berth curtains there began to appear an assortment of human heads.

Above the scene there sounded the flutter of beating wings.

The Backslid Baptist dived into the centre of the Pullman.

"What is it, porter?"

"Jes' gittin' into Carbondale." The porter's calm voice dispelled the terrors of the night.

"Leggo! Leggo! Doggone you. Backslid! Come heah!"

A furore of acrobatic groaning marked a scene wherein the Wildcat was doing the best he could to pry himself loose from something that clung to various parts of his anatomy with a beak and eight sharp claws.

"Come heah! Light de light. Some varmint's got me."

The Backslid Baptist retraced his steps. "Ain't no varmint. One ob dem parrot birds."

The Backslid Baptist made a grab for the parrot, and from the bird's throat into the night again there lifted the wild laughter.

The porter opened the door of the linen closet wherein Lily the mascot goat was quietly eating her third pillow case. He cast the parrot from him into the darkness of the linen closet. "Wilecat, tell de lady in Lo' 10 Ah'll take keer de parrot till mawin'."

The parrot landed on Lily's neck. From behind the slammed door came a muffled "Blaa!" followed by the subdued noises of a large number-nine-sized ruckus.

Zing! Zing! ZING!

"I's coming. I's coming." The Backslid Baptist filled two cups of ice-water and started toward Lower 7 with them.

"Heah you is.... Yessuh. No suh. Yessuh, Ah'll git you some mo'."

"Here's a half bottle of that blasted stuff. Take it away where I can't smell it. That ice-water sure is good. Were you ever zippo on gin?"

"No suh. Ah'll git you some mo' ice-water."

The Backslid Baptist, conveying half a bottle of gin, neglected to state that he had never been able to accumulate enough gin at one time to get himself zippo.

He encountered the Wildcat in the smoking room. He handed the Wildcat the half bottle of gin. "Ah'll say I's a mind reader."

"See whut de good Lawd done sent!"

"Afteh de storm comes de quiet waters."

"Comes de gin, you means. Ol' fat boy drink de watehs. Us drinks de gin. Gin, how is you?"

The Wildcat soothed himself with three strenuous gulps. "Whuf! Liquor, how de do!"

The Backslid Baptist departed with the third cargo of ice-water for the gentleman in Lower 7. He returned after a little while. Dangling from his fingers and carried in his arms were a dozen pairs of shoes.

He threw the shoes down on the end seat in the smoking room. "Start to work on de shoes, Wilecat. Don' do nothin' to de new shoes--much--an' hit de ol' ones light. De middle-grade shoes gits a good shinin'. Folks whut weahs middle-grade shoes is ol'-time travellers an' gin'ally comes up strong wid de income tax fo' us boys."

The bell in the passageway sounded its summons.

"Doggone! See who dat is."

The apprenticed Wildcat read the indicator. "Ain't no numbeh. De little hand turned on de letters."

"Whut de letters say?"

"Backslid, you knows I kain't read."

The Backslid Baptist set the nearly empty bottle of gin on the washstand and walked into the passageway.

"'Partment B," he announced upon his return. "Dey's two 'partments, A and B, and a drawin' room. You knows 'B' when you sees it. Knock at de do' an' ask whut is it."

The Wildcat departed on his mission. At the door of Compartment B he encountered a bald-headed gentleman clad in violent pink pajamas. The gentleman's face was festooned with a long, blond mustache. He thrust a coat, a vest, and a pair of trousers through the door at the Wildcat.

"Have these pressed," he ordered. "Here's a brace of shillings for you. Fee the tailor chap."

"Cap'n, yessuh."

The Wildcat returned to the smoking room. "Boy in de 'partment room whut gobbles lak a turkey says, 'Press de clo'es, boy, an' heah's a dollah.' Dollah, how is you? Sho' is easy money."

"English boy. Dey's de clo'es-pressin'est folks in de world, 'ceptin' actors."

"Whah at does I git dese fixed up?"

"No place. Hang de coat up. Sprinkle de pants wid wateh an' lay 'em undeh a pile ob sheets in de linen closet. By mornin' dey's pressed. You charges anotheh dollah."

"Sho' is easy money." The Wildcat hung the Britisher's coat and vest in the smoking room. He walked into the passageway and opened the door of the linen closet. A four-legged cyclone burst from the dark depths of the linen closet. Riding the cyclone was a bedraggled parrot. The parrot showed the wear and tear of travel.

The Wildcat called loudly at the cyclone.

"Lily, halt! 'Tenshun! Whah at's de mil'tary bearin' you got in France? Come heah!"

The mascot walked to the Wildcat's side. From Lily's cringing back the Wildcat lifted the battle-scarred parrot.

The Wildcat boosted Lily back into the solitude of the linen closet. "Lily, 'tenshun. At ease! At res'!"

The goat executed the commands with the military precision which had come from long months of training in the A.E.F.

"'Tenshun! At ease. One mo' false move an' I th'ows you oveh-boa'd off de train."

The Wildcat retrieved a piece of string and turned his attention to the parrot. "You green debbil. Lay off 'at goat. Ah ties you on de top shelf. One mo' move an' us has fricasseed green chicken afteh de dinin' cah man gits you."

"'Tenshun!" mocked the parrot. "At ease!" Lily, prone in the depths of the linen closet, obeyed the commands.

The Wildcat tied the string around the parrot's leg. "Dere, dat holds you, an quit mockin' me befo' I knocks yo' beak down yo' throat."

"At rest!" the parrot gurgled.

The Wildcat closed the door of the linen closet. The parrot lost no time in biting the string loose from about her leg, after which she rejoined her four-legged companion.

"'Tenshun!" she squawked. "At res'! Tenshun! At res'!"

Thereafter until dawn, obeying the perfect counterfeit of her master's voice, Lily the mascot goat came to attention and subsided at rest with the persistent rhythm of a man on a hand-car.

CHAPTER VI

The Wildcat returned to his shoe-shining. "When does us boys sleep, Backslid?" "When de chance comes," the Backslid Baptist returned. "You sleeps between stations an' 'twixt jobs of work. Gin'ally when de bell rings at night you pay no 'tenshun to it. Folks is finicky. Dey gits along just de same does you answer de bell or don't you. Hurry up wid de shoes. When you gits 'em done come on up th'ee cahs ahead. Dey's some res'less ivory on dat cah, an' mebbe us collects some money whut's lonesome to change managers."

The Backslid Baptist departed for the third car ahead, where in the smoking room the galloping ivory was clicking strong on the linoleum.

The Wildcat finished his work on the shoes of the passengers on the Mazeppa. He carried the shoes forward with him until he came upon the crap game.

"Heah's de shoes, Backslid," he said. "Men, howdy."

"Whut fo' you bring dem shoes all de way up heah?"

"Ah kain't read yo' numbehs whah at to distribute 'em."

"Lay 'em down. Ah'll take 'em back afteh while. Gimme dem bones. Shoots five dollahs." The Backslid Baptist launched himself into an energetic arm-swinging struggle, wherein presently he lost after his third pass.

"Take a ra'r, Wilecat. See is you still 'fested wid luck like you wuz in de A.E.F."

The Wildcat was a stranger to everybody present except the Backslid Baptist.

"Who dat boy?" one of the group of porters asked.

"Learnin' boy f'm Memphis. Ah knows him." With this endorsement the Wildcat was plunged into the game.

"Gimme dem bones. Hind laigs at res'." The Wildcat subsided to the floor. "Fingehs, lemme see kin you play de pickpocket jazz. Shoots five dollahs. Wham! Ah reads a feeble five. Five stay alive. Five Ah craves. Lady Luck, boon me. P'odigal five, come home whah de fat calf waits. Bam! Th'ee an' a deuce. Ah lets it lay. Shoots ten dollahs. Shower down ten dollahs an' see de train robbeh perform. Shower down, brothers. Bam! Seven! 'At's twins, but mah luck comes triple. Shoots de twenty. Shoots twenty dollahs. Heah de bloodhoun' bay. An' Ah reads ten miles. Chicago bound! Pay day, whah at is you? Lady Luck, don' git feeble. Angil leanin' on a cloud. De cloud busts! Angil, heah you is--readin' de five an' five. Five twins, how is you? Shoots fo'ty dollahs."

One of the group spoke to the Backslid. "Mebbe 'at boy's learnin' de porter business, but he sho' got old in de bone school a long time back."

The Backslid Baptist grunted his reply.

The Wildcat raked down all of his winnings except a five-dollar bill. "Shoots five dollahs. Shower down. Windy talk don't shake no possums loose. Come an' git me on de top limb. Shoots five dollahs. Dynamite dice, bust de ol' safe do'. Ah craves action. Shoots ten dollahs. Fifty dollahs."

"How much you got?" A cinnamon-coloured Croesus in the group spoke softly into the clamour.

The Wildcat turned to him. "Shoots a hund'ed does you crave speed. Shoots five hund'ed dollahs."

The cinnamon-faced porter produced a roll of bills and stripped a handful of greenbacks therefrom.

"'At's five hund'ed dollahs. Roll 'em."

"Gallopers, git right."

The Wildcat gave the dice a Turkish bath, a manicure, and a careful massaging between the perspiring palms of his hands.

He cast a handful of prepared ivory from him. The dice were festooned with equal parts of luck and technical skill, but their precise trajectory was interrupted by a string of high joints and low centres in the track over which rambled the Panama Limited.

"An' I reads--ace and deuce."

The cinnamon-coloured boy picked up the money on the floor.

"'At'll learn you."

The Wildcat was silent. The Backslid Baptist, sharing the shadow of his associate's sudden cloud of black luck, spoke slowly to him.

"C'm on heah, Wilecat. Us is nex' do' to bein' busted."

In the wake of the Backslid Baptist the Wildcat ambled back through the swaying cars to the Mazeppa. He carried on his bowed shoulders a load of misery big enough to bust a bottle of dynamite gin.

The Backslid Baptist stretched himself full length on the long leather seat of the smoking room.

"Baptist, how come it I don' know. De baby gallopehs wuz spinnin' fo' seven."

"Rough track an' de rocky road swerved 'em. Git to sleep. Us is due at Champaign at 8:10. Money come, money go. Whuteveh sleep you gits is that much to de good."

The Wildcat flopped down on the floor of the smoking room, but sleep would not come to him.

At half past seven the Backslid Baptist on the leather seat began mumbling to himself. A little later he awakened.

"Wilecat, whut dat noise?"

"Ain't heard no noise." All the Wildcat had heard was the accents of his bank-roll bidding him a last farewell.

"'At thumpin' noise." The Backslid Baptist's ears, keenly attuned to the turmoil of travel, distinguished in the sounds about him some unfamiliar puncture of the normal din.

"Sounded lak beatin' a board wid a stick."

"Kain't heah nothin'."

The Backslid Baptist yawned. "Some ob dem early risers f'm de tall sticks sure to be up by now. When Ah starts makin' up de berths you kin sweep out de cah an' 'cumulate de sheets an' pillow cases. Stick 'em in de canvas bag in de linen closet an' take back de boy's clo'es he gin you to press."

The Wildcat traversed the length of the aisle back of a swinging broom. On the return trip he encountered the Backslid Baptist busily engaged in making up Lower 1.

"Backslid, who dem two boys half way down de cah wid de red hats?"

"You means de boys wid de red fezants? Dem's a couple ob Potent Nobles ob de Mysterious Mecca. All de Mysterious Mecca boys in de world is havin' a gran' ruckus next month on de Pacific Coast."

"How come dey start so early?"

"Dey falls by de wayside heah an' dere, an' dey starts early so as to git picked up by some worthy Brother wid steady laigs. 'At fat boy wid de red fezant is de one whut had de gin hiccoughs."

"Kain't see did he."

"Gin'ally dey carries it noble. Dere's de little lady whut owns de parrot bird."

The owner of the parrot bird was a left-over soubrette who had bust in Havana with a road production of The Sillies of 1492. The little lady had completed her spring drinking and was now en route to a big-time meal-ticket scheduled to start from Chicago.

She saw the Wildcat.

"Porter, where is little Polly?"

"Yessum. I secluded 'at green chicken in de linen closet. Does you crave him now?"

"Yes. I want to have her with me for breakfast--the poor lonesome darling."

"Accordin' to de words 'at varmint used last night, he's too tough to make much of a brekfus'."

The Wildcat went to the end of the car and opened the linen closet wherein he had cached the parrot.

With the opening of the door the mystery of the thumping noise which he and the Backslid Baptist had heard was explained. In a low falsetto the parrot was repeating the two military commands which she had learned.

"'Tenshun! At res'! 'Tenshun! At res'!"

Lily, the mascot goat, was contributing the last fragment of muscular energy to the business of obeying orders. In response to the parrot's commands the goat languidly flopped at rest on the floor of the linen closet and came to her feet at attention.

"Lawd Gawd, Lily! At res' an' stay 'at way!"

Gratitude rang in the answering "Blaa" of Lily the goat.

The Wildcat reached for the parrot. "You green debbil! Whut you mean, exercisin' mah mascot all night?"

"Quawk!" The parrot made a vicious swing at the Wildcat's reaching hand.

"Leggo, you debbil!"

The green parrot, fuming in a rage compared to which nitric acid was a cream puff, was restored to its Spring-drinking owner.

"Lady, heah's de green demon."

"Pretty Polly. What made her little feathers all mussed up?"

The Wildcat returned to his exhausted mascot.

"'At green chicken's lucky does he git by widout gittin' his health an' stren'th mussed up befo' dis trip ends. At res', Lily, till I brings you some nutriment. Doggone ol' bird must have near wore you out. 'At's de way wid dem mil'tary commands. Res' yo'se'f, Lily, till Ah brings yo' brekfust."

"Blaa!" answered Lily, weakly.

The Wildcat detected a tone of hypocrisy,--something of false gratitude--in the mascot's reply. He returned from the dining car carrying two heads of lettuce for the mascot. He placed the lettuce under the nose of the recumbent goat, but Lily refused to eat.

"Fust time Ah eveh seed you slow up when de mess call blowed. How come?"

An instant later his roving eye discovered the "how come" of Lily's loss of appetite. In a dark corner of the linen closet he saw a dozen fragments of white cloth. He hauled them out, and the light revealed the hems of a covey of sheets and a half dozen pillow cases. Then the web of a home-spun disaster met his eye. From the lower shelf of the linen closet dangled the shredded legs of the trousers which the occupant of Compartment B had given him to be pressed.

"Goat, doggone you, come to 'tenshun! No wondeh you kain't eat lettuce, wid yo' insides crammed wid a ton ob linen an' half a pair ob pants fo' dessert. Me sympathizin' wid you, an' you an' de green chicken banquetin' all night on 'spensive raiment! 'Ceptin' foh havin' to scrub de flo', I'd barbecue de blood outen yo' veins heah an' now."

The sudden necessity of hiding the evidence confronted the Wildcat.

"By rights I ought to ram de rest ob de pants down yo' neck." The Wildcat picked up the ragged and frazzled trousers. A moment later he opened the door of the car platform and cast the remnants of Lily's banquet into the fleeting right-of-way.

"'Spect some boy find dese an' say, 'Whah at's de man whut de train cut de laigs off of?' 'At's his trouble. Me--Ah's Chicago bound wid a cahload ob trouble ob mah own. Main thing to do is to git off de train widout lettin' 'at boy in 'partment B know we's landed."

He discussed the disaster of the trousers with the Backslid Baptist.

"'At's de on'y way," the porter conceded. "When us gits in we fo'gits 'bout de boy widout de pants. Dey wuz his pants, Wilecat. Havin' no pants is his grief. He kin borrow some overalls f'm de cah cleaners, o' else he kin play he's a Injun an' roam nekked till de police gits him. Does us meet up wid de ol' Pullman 'spector Ah says 'No suh, Ah dunno how come.' 'At's 'at."

"Sho' don't crave words wid no 'spector," the Wildcat returned. "Dis porter business de best job in de world. Ridin' all de time, seem' de country--eatin' heavy, free ice wateh, gran' raiment, talkin' to folks--No suh! Main thing Ah craves is to git hired by de Pullman boss. 'Spect Ah makes it all right, Baptis'?"

"You makes it easy. You's done learned de business dis mawnin', ain't you? Well, I gits you five recommendin' letters f'm a boy whut writes 'em on Prairie Avenue, an' you gits hired.

"Fust letter says, 'Ah knowed Wilecat goin' on ten yeahs, an' he don't drink.' Nex' letter say, 'Wilecat jined de church when he wuz four yeahs old an' bin a soldier ob de Lawd eveh since.' Nex' letter say, 'Boy got to take keer ob his wife, mother an' father, an' six small chillen.' Nex' letter say, 'Wilecat sho' beats de worl' fo' readin', writin', an' 'rithmetic.'"

"Backslid, you knows Ah kain't read."

"'At don't make no difference. Letter says so, don't it? Last letter says you's honest, industrious, an reli'ble."

"How come you so friendly wid dat Democrat letter-writin' boy?"

"How come 'Democrat'?"

"F'm whut you says he's champion liar ob de world. Sounds Democrat to me. Don' make no difference, though--just so's I gits de job."

CHAPTER VII

Zing!

The owner of the red fez and the night-blooming hiccoughs craved another pillow and a table. The Wildcat delivered the table and fixed it into place. He returned to the linen closet to retrieve a pillow case therefrom. When the door opened, Lily the mascot goat, tired of the dark confines of her retreat, burst forth and galloped down the aisle of the car.

The Wildcat abandoned his pillow case industry and spent the next two minutes in rounding up his protege.

"You ramblin' wreck, come back heah befo' Ah makes a rug out ob yo' skin."

He returned Lily to her jail and proceeded to deliver the second pillow to the owner of the alcohol snorts. In common with the rest of the occupants of the car, that individual voiced his curiosity concerning the animated mascot.

"Son, who owns the goat?"

"Cap'n, suh, Ah owns him now, but some slaughter house man gwine to git him 'less he ca'ms down."

"What'll you take for him?"

The Wildcat suddenly remembered his financial status. Hard money at the moment made a strong appeal.

"Cap'n, suh, you means you craves to buy 'at goat?"

In the mind of the Potent Noble of the Mysterious Mecca had bloomed a Great Idea, wherein the galloping Lily would provide entertainment in carload lots for the Convention-bound brethren of the Conclave.

"Some days Ah'd sell 'at goat fo' a thin dime. Otheh days Ah'd give a boy a hund'ed dollahs for killin' him."

"What'll you take for him cash down, f.o.b. Lower 7, car Mazeppa?"

The Wildcat studied for a moment, and then long months of association clinched the tie which Lady Luck had woven between him and the prodigal Lily.

"Cap'n, suh, Ah spec' Ah wouldn't sell 'at goat fo' mo'n a million dollahs. Me an' Lily fit so many battles togetheh in France and on boa'd de ol' iron boat comin' home 'at Ah kain't see no money big enough to 'suage mah grief is we divo'ced. Bible says, 'Whither the goat goes, me too.' 'Spec Ah kain't sell him."

The companion Noble across the table from the hiccoughing gentleman offered a suggestion. "Round 'em both up for the trip. The Pullman gang'll fix it for us."

"Good scheme, Jim. The old bean isn't any too clear this morning or I'd thought of that myself." The owner of the red fezant turned to the Wildcat.

"What's your name, son?"

"Dey named me Marsden, suh--Vitus Marsden--but folks calls me Wilecat."

"If I can't buy the goat, I guess we'll have to negotiate the custody of your feline corpus from the Pullman organization for the duration of the Big Show."

"Yessuh." The Wildcat did not understand the big words, but whenever he did not understand it was his principle to smile and agree to anything that white gentlemen said.

"Yessuh. Ain't it de truf'?" He returned to the smoking compartment, where the Backslid Baptist was auditing his tips.

The Backslid Baptist was busy at the moment excavating a busted cork out of the neck of a queer looking square bottle.

"Baptis', whut you got?"

"Smells lak equalizer. Wait till Ah gits dis cork out, an' us sees."

"Whut dat sign say on de bottle?"

The Backslid Baptist inspected the label affixed to the flat side of the bottle. "Ol' sign reads 'Acrobatic Spirits of Pneumonia.' Bam! Un-konkered de ol' cork. Smell dat. 'At learns you not to believe in

signs. When yo' eyes sees one thing an' yo' nose sees another you
betteh believe yo' nose." He took a long drag at the bottle and passed
it over to the Wildcat.

"Whuf! Ol' lady in Lower 6 felt poo'ly dis mawnin', but she 'sorbed
th'ee drams f'm dis heah bottle, an' so far she's et twelve dollahs'
wuth ob grub up ahaid in de dinin' cah."

The Wildcat swung on to the "Acrobatic Spirits of Pneumonia," lingering
at the spout for several disappointing seconds after the contents of
the bottle had gurgled down his neck.

"Whuf! Ah missed de pneumonia, Backslid, but Ah sho' feels acrobatic.
How come de lady lose de bottle?"

"She done got careless when de spirits come. You better th'o 'at
glassware away now an' git ready fo' tellin' de boss how you craves a
porter's job."

Half an hour later, leading his mascot goat and closely convoyed by the
Backslid Baptist, the Wildcat walked down the platform in the dark
trainshed of the station in Chicago. Throughout the long ride down
Prairie Avenue to the habitation of the forger from whom the
recommending letters were to be obtained the Wildcat's woolly bean spun
with the momentum which he had drained from the bottle abandoned by the
careless lady in Lower 6.

An hour later, armed with five ironclad letters, he returned along the
route, arriving finally at the portals of the office building on West
Adams Street wherein Pullman porters are created from select brunet
humanity.

Presently, across a wide desk he confronted Authority. A kindly gentleman questioned him, and to the questions he replied with an assortment of impromptu lies whose range and ingenuity busted every previous record for careless language.

Ten minutes later he was a hired man.

"C'm on heah. 'At's all." The Backslid Baptist at his elbow sensed the successful conclusion of the interview.

"You mean Ah's a porter?" the bewildered Wildcat asked when the pair had gained the street level.

"Ah'll say you is."

"An' all de tips I gits is mine to keep?"

"Dey is previdin' you gits outen yo' trance an' takes yo' cah on de 4:10."

"Hot dam, Lily! C'm on heah. Us weahs a blue coat all de time an' don't do nuthin' but spend de money whut de white folks showers down."

"You betteh make arrangements at some livery stable to p'vide board an' room fo' Lily whilst you is A.W.O.L."

"How come? Whah at I goes de goat goes."

"Not on de Pullman run. Ah dead-heads you once, an' de goat lak to ruined eve'ybody in de cah. No suh! Kain't run no trains an' no mascot at de same time. De rule book leaves out goats, but does you lug Lily wid you, yo' fust run sho' is yo' last."

The Wildcat faced the moment of a great decision. "Den dey won't be no

fust trip. Cm on heah, Lily. Much 'bliged, Baptis'. Me an' Lily looks
fo' a job whah at dey ain't no rules again' mascots."

The Wildcat headed south along Michigan Avenue, and in a little while
he and Lily were adrift in a sea of humanity.

The Backslid Baptist grunted his disgust and went about his own
affairs.

CHAPTER VIII

At midnight the Wildcat and Lily pitched their lonely camp behind a
billboard in South Chicago.

"Sho' craves mah rations. You done noble wid de grass, Lily, but Ah
kain't eat grass. Seems lak you kin nutrify yo'se'f wid whuteveh
vittles is laying 'round."

In the dawn the Wildcat realized that his appetite had sprung up like a
mushroom over night.

"Wisht us wuz back wid ol' Cap'n Jack in Memphis, whah at de ham-tree
blooms th'ee times a day."

At noon his stomach was the residence of a hunger panic. With his
mascot trailing behind him, he headed toward the heart of the city.

"Doggone 'at crap-shootin' hound. How come he clean me to mah last
nickel, Ah don' know. Lady Luck, whah at is you?"

An instant later, wearing a policeman's uniform and speaking a wild Irish language, Lady Luck descended upon the Wildcat. The Michigan Avenue traffic cop abandoned his post long enough to pounce upon his prey.

"What th' hell do yez mean prowlin' round th' Loop in broad daylight wid ivery man on th' force goin' crazy lookin' f'r yez? Come along wid me."

Ten minutes later, with the echoes of the patrol gong still ringing in his ears, the Wildcat and Lily were hazed through the black portals of an unfriendly looking police station. They faced the desk sergeant.

"Boy, is your name Vitus Marsden?"

"Cap'n, yessuh. Folks gin'ally calls me Wilecat."

The desk sergeant busied himself with the telephone at his elbow. Two minutes later he turned to the Wildcat.

"Sit on that bench over there," he said.

The Wildcat sat down, and a black cloud of surmise floated across his immediate horizon.

"Lily, Ah 'spect us is 'rested mebbe on 'count ob dem pants you et offen de man in old 'partment B. Mebbe I'se took fo' 'sorbin' dem Acrobatic Spirits whut Backslid consecrated to me. Mebbe de lady wid de green chicken whut you et de feathers off ob done craved revenge. Mebbe de ol' Pullman car man aims to make you work out de price of 'at laundry you et in de linen closet."

The Wildcat had no difficulty finding a dozen good reasons for his present embarrassment. He addressed a police officer near by.

"Cap'n suh, whut fo' is me an' Lily sequestered heah in de jail?"

Before the policeman could answer, the march of events made reply. Through the swinging doors of the station filed a dozen strange looking men. These men wore baggy red trousers, and on each man's head was the red fez which marked him as being a Potent Noble of the Mysterious Mecca.

They descended upon the Wildcat. "Come on here, boy. Bring that goat. You and the mascot are due out on our special train twenty minutes from now. Here's your orders from the Pullman Company. You're on the payroll, and so is the mascot goat."

"Cap'n, suh, you means me an' Lily is headed west wid de red fezant gen'men?"

"That's it."

"Hot dam! Lily, 'tenshun! Lady Luck, how come I doubt you?"

CHAPTER IX

The Wildcat expanded in the sunlight of Lady Luck's smile.

"Lady Luck, how come I doubt you? Police folks, good-bye. Lily, 'tenshun! Come on heah. Us is a Pullman poteh. Ah craves mah rest. Le's go."

Surrounded by an escort of Potent Nobles of the Mysterious Mecca, the Wildcat marched from the portals of the Chicago police station, headed for a west-bound train wherein he aimed to do the best he could in the role of porter for his carload of nobles.

At the train gates the party was delayed five minutes to permit the entrance of a motley crew of manacled aliens.

"How come them boys festooned with so much jinglin' hardware?"

One of the Potent Nobles made reply.

"Bad actors."

"Cap'n, suh, who's dat black boy wid de straight hair and his head tied up in de white rag?"

"Hindoo."

"Some boy sho' must ob busted his head open, to need tyin' up so bad."

Following the line of undesirables headed away from the land of the free, Lily, the Wildcat, and the Potent Nobles filtered through the gates into the train shed. They made their way down a long string of coaches, arriving finally at the Mazeppa.

"Here's the car."

"Car, howdy. Lily, git aboa'd."

"Slip out and get me a box of cigars before we leave."

A Potent Noble shoved a banknote at the Wildcat.

"Cap'n, yessuh. Would you mind tyin' Lily on de front vegetable ob de car till I gits back?"

Twelve minutes later, carrying in his hand a box of cigars, the Wildcat's second entrance was blocked by a ticket chopper who had a square jaw and a sense of duty.

"Where's your ticket?"

"Ain't got no ticket. I's de poteh wid de Mysterious Mecca gen'men. Le' me by."

"Don't try to pull none o' that stuff around me."

"Man, leave me by!"

Armed with the conviction of authority and clad in a parade-leading Prince Albert whose brass buttons reassured him, the Wildcat violated one of the first principles of his life, which was never to oppose a white man. He slid past the ticket chopper, ducked into the gate, and boarded the train wherein rolled the Mazeppa. He caught a tourist Pullman three cars apart from the rolling residence of the Mysterious Mecca delegation and landed breathless in the open vestibule.

"Fust thing old Backslid, what learned me de po'teh bizness, said to do was to close up de vegetable."

This he proceeded to do. He turned and entered the car. For a second time he slid past blue-coated authority, in the form of a United States Deputy Marshal who was temporarily chaperoning the departing aliens.

"Hold on, there: where you headed for?"

"I's de poteh what takes care ob de Noble Fezant boys in de blue
pants."

The deputy marshal temporarily on guard had a fixed official rule of
conduct: never take a chance. The Wildcat's words sounded crazy enough
to entitle him to a membership card in the Traveling Nut Club.

"Git in that car and sit down before I blow your head off! Where's your
handcuffs?"

"Cap'n, how come? Handcuffs seems so confidential."

Here, for some reason unknown to the Wildcat, was the hand of the law.
Inside of his parade-leading Prince Albert the Wildcat shivered and
shrunk three sizes. His brow wrinkled in perplexity beneath the velvet
hat, and the bright yellow plumes thereon dropped in sudden melancholy.

"Lady Luck, whah at is you?"

"Mumblin' to himself and wearing the craziest rig in the car--good
thing I rounded up that bird."

The deputy marshal added another star to his crown. "Plumb bughouse."

He cast his eye over the occupants of the car. "Back to Russia. Try
some of your ideas on them Bullshevik birds."

He again addressed the Wildcat.

"Cut out that mumblin'. All you got to do is keep still."

"Cap'n, yessuh." The Wildcat removed his velvet hat and subsided in a seat beside the Hindoo agitator.

"How come you got your head all tied up, boy?" he asked the Hindoo.

The Anarchist didn't see fit to reply.

At Omaha the guards from the western division relieved their homesick eastern brothers.

"Twenty-three of them," announced the man who had captured the Wildcat. "Watch that rag-head Hindoo and that nigger in the fourth seat. He's gittin' bad, all the time mumblin' to himself about Lady Luck and Lily; he believes he's a porter."

Over the miles official carelessness rode in the carload of bad actors. Only when the train stopped were the guards vigilant.

Sagged down in his seat beside the Hindoo, the Wildcat reviewed a tolerably measly past.

"How come?"

There was no accounting for what white men would do to a boy, but somewhere in the jumble the Wildcat sensed that he had been the victim of a mistake.

"Mebbe I's headed fo' jail 'count o' runnin' past de man at de gates."

After a thirty-minute delay at Granger the Wildcat saw a train leave the yards. On the platform of the observation car, surrounded by half a dozen Blue Fezant Nobles of the Mysterious Mecca, he saw Lily speeding away into an isolated future.

"Lily, you hoodoo, good-bye. Lady Luck, here I is."

CHAPTER X

1.

In the early days of detachable cuffs and ten-cent whisky there had been a difference of opinion manifest in the railroad surveying party at Granger.

Part of the gang headed northward to the salmon country; the rest of them blazed a trail to the southwest, where the sand fleas live on artichokes.

Lily and her escort were headed southwest towards San Francisco. Presently the Wildcat's car was cut into a train whose trail led northward through Idaho and Oregon.

Lady Luck meanwhile had a hard time keeping up. Exhausted finally with her efforts, she set the stage a few hundred miles ahead and lay down and went to sleep. While she was sleeping a pair of hard boiled actors in the drama rummaged around in the woodshed back of a log house near the banks of the Columbia river.

Pete, a skinny character with ears like a loving cup, raked three wheat sacks out of a pile of lumber.

Into two of these sacks he cut a pair of holes two inches in diameter and about four inches apart. The third sack he left intact. He handed one of the sacks to his partner.

"Here she is; see if it fits you."

A fat bad actor by the name of Bill slipped the sack over his head. "Little narrow between the eyes."

Three hours later these two agents of Lady Luck engaged in a little hard work in their search for easy money. The product of their energy took shape in the form of a pyramid of old ties piled between the rails of the line over which the Wildcat was approaching in his twelve-wheeled cage.

Ten minutes before the train was due and while her crossing whistles could be heard in the dusk five miles up-stream, the two bad actors scrambled up the south bank of the Columbia. The skinny one poured a quart bottle of coal oil on the pile of ties and lighted it. The fat man lighted a cigarette.

Both of them drew the wheat sacks over their heads. The fat man carried the third wheat sack slung at his waist on a string which went around his shoulder.

The stillness of evening was broken by the roar of a locomotive whistle, and an instant later the wheels of the train smoked and screeched against the chattering brake shoes. In the cab ahead the handle of the air valve was slammed into the big notch.

The flagman swung down from the rear end of the train and ambled back along the track for half the regulation distance. He set his lantern in the middle of the track and rolled a cigarette. Three lanterns flashed along the train, where the train countered a locked door. Inside the car, on a seat to see what was going on.

Presently they found out and took their places beside the fireman and engineer, hands raised.

With his wheat sack dangling more heavily on his hip as he progressed through the train, the fat bad actor skimmed the Pullman cream on his way forward to the plated jewelry in the day coach.

On the vestibule of the Wildcat's car he encountered a locked door. Inside the car, on a seat beside the rag-head Hindoo, the Wildcat curled himself up as a preface to twelve long chapters of easy sleep.

"Sho's noble when de train stops; boy can sleep peaceful 'thout gittin' his insides scrambled."

"Bam!"

The fat bad actor shot the lock off the door of the Wildcat's car.

"Boy sure can sleep noble. Good mawnin--"

The rest of the sentence was action and not words. On the echo of the shot from the fat bad actor's gun the Wildcat leaped automatically. He ran fast enough to sidestep two more shots that crashed into the night after him. The Hindoo passed him in the darkness.

Down along the track the Wildcat's feet tore up great gobs of right-of-way. He passed the flagman, going like a brunet typhoon ten days overdue. After the first mile he began putting his feet down a little slower before he stepped on them. At the second mile his hind legs were dragging, and then suddenly, instead of the hard ground beneath his feet, there was nothing but a black void.

He rolled a few times like a 'possum falling off a limb. He landed on the hard sand of the river bank. Night had fallen.

"Lady Luck, here us is. Whah at is we?"

The Wildcat curled up and went to sleep.

He woke up five minutes later. "Sho' is peaceful. How come I's so thirsty?"

Beside him the river offered him a solution to his thirst problems. On all fours he crawled to the river edge. He shoved his bow under the water and nearly sank himself absorbing as much of the Columbia river as could flow into his wide mouth.

"Whuff! Sho' is noble water."

The black rippling water before him was suddenly shot with silver. Then it became a solid glistening black. A school of smelt, seeking the quiet water of the bank, fought their way upstream. The Wildcat reached a tentative exploring paw into the stream of fish.

"Fish, howdy. De table sho' is set. Come out heah."

With his bare hands he snatched ashore a breakfast four sizes too big for his optimistic estimate of his stomach's capacity.

"Quit floppin'. Ole Wilecat's done caught you." He felt for the box of Pullman matches in the pocket of his shirt, beneath the folds of the parade-leading Prince Albert. Here was food and a chance to sleep. With the Wildcat, all was well.

He accumulated a pile of firewood from the river bank, and presently a
great fire was blazing. For an hour he gorged himself on smelt.

"Whuff! Sho's noble fish. Now I sees kin I sleep me."

The twinkling stars rattled in their orbits in cadence to the Wildcat's
snores. Sufficient unto the night was the evil thereof. Here, except
for a few sand fleas, was peace. The Wildcat snuggled deeper into the
intimate environment of the sand about him. His lower jaw dropped, and
his tongue lolled out less than a foot. Three or four mosquitoes landed
on him and did a little boring, but the Wildcat slept on. Presently the
halo of fish about him quit flopping. In the dark waters of the river's
margin their myriad brethren fought their way upstream. The Wildcat
mumbled in his sleep,

> "Lady Luck sure done noble.
> I sleeps mos' all de time.
> I don' give a dog-gone
> If de sun don't nevah shine."

2.

In the Cascades there had been berries enough for the bears and for the
Indians. Now that the salmon run was heralded in the Columbia by the
little fish scouts, all of the scattered members of the Flathead tribe
not otherwise engaged coagulated from their several loafing grounds and
headed for Memloose Island to pay their annual respects to the ghost of
the King Salmon.

Included in the tribe were a few solid citizens. Some of these were
college graduates. John Running Bear, better known to the business men

of The Dalles as John Franklin, left his tailored clothes at home and painted his brown body with yellow ochre. He stained his arms and face with the tribal marks of his people. He drove in his twelve-cylinder car to a point near the upstream tip of Memloose Island, whereon the Flathead salmon dance was to be held. He parked his car in a thicket of willows.

"Safe enough," he said to his companion. "If some bundle-stiff or some drifter from a sheep camp up the line needs the old wagon more than I do, he's welcome to it. Let's go."

At dawn Running Bear and his companions encountered a hundred of their fellows. From the camp the smoke of the cooking fires lifted in the still air. Running Bear opened a tin of chicken. He sighed.

"This is the last civilized meal for the next six days."

He breakfasted slowly, lingering over his coffee, and then half reluctantly the last trace of civilization's veneer was cast aside.

"Clee Hy Yah Skookum Kum chuck. Waugh!"

3.

Half a mile upstream from the Indian camp the Wildcat greeted the dawn. Building a quick fire, he looked about him at the wrinkled little fish, drying in the early morning sunlight. Slithering past him in the water still persisted the mad rush of racing myriads. He threw the dead fish back into the stream and raked out a fresher breakfast.

He poulticed a dozen fish with maple leaves and threw them in the glowing coals of his fire. Ten minutes later he again began the business of gorging himself on free fish.

"Don't cost me nuthin'." He clawed the water for another dozen handfuls. "Free fish, howdy doo.

> "I eats when I can git it.
> I sleeps mos' all de time."

Gorged to the bursting point, the Wildcat rolled over in the warm sunlight. He preferred not to go to sleep again, but in five minutes he was snoring along at his old sixty-mile gait. He slept all day.

He was discovered and surrounded at evening by Running Bear and the rest of the tribe.

Running Bear sized up the situation and pulled off a pow-wow with three or four of his companions. They arrived at a verdict.

"A little black-face vaudeville might liven things up. These blasted tribal ceremonies need a cabaret attachment to jazz them up. How about it, redskins?"

"Let's go."

The verdict was unanimous.

Somewhere in the Wildcat's dreams there presently developed a rhythm in which the cadence of dancing feet punctuated his slumbers. His eyes opened finally, and within the range of his vision passed a parade of leaping figures. To his ears came the regular booming beat of a deerskin tom-tom, punctuated by an occasional blood-curdling yell.

His memory failed him.

"How come dis voodoo bizness?"

He sat up. He got to his feet and instinctively crouched to a running position.

The ring of dancing warriors about him tightened up.

"Lady Luck, whah is you?"

Running Bear lifted a flint-tipped spear over his head and emitted a shriek compared to which the Rebel yell was a chirp from the weakened lungs of the dove of peace.

In spite of his fish-distended anatomy, the Wildcat shrivelled to boy's size.

Running Bear emitted several mouthfuls of language.

"Naw suh, not me." The Wildcat denied everything. "I ain't only a field han'. Lemme by, boy. Whah at's yo' pants? How come you runnin' around nekked?"

"Waugh!"

Six Indians seized the Wildcat, and a moment later he was seated in the stern of a twenty-foot skiff, which presently embarked upon the surface of the Columbia. Beside the Wildcat sat Running Bear, speaking a fluent mixture of Flathead and Chinook.

In time with Running Bear's measured periods, the Wildcat rolled his eyes. Now and then when the Indian's sense of humour got the best of him he varied his Chinook jargon with Wild shrieks of laughter.

"Sounds like dem crazy folks in dat car comin' from Chicago. Seems like de whole worl' done got crowded wid fools. What you laffin' at, boy?"

In a little while the party landed at Memloose Island. Before them, rising sharply against the evening sky, drooping cottonwoods lifted high above an undergrowth of willows. The party marched down a little trail for half the length of the island, and then, at a point where the trail divided into the sombre interior of the wooded terrain, they left the sunlight.

After a march of a hundred yards they came upon a clearing. About the clearing in the fringing woods were fifty rickety structures lifted on poles. On each of these, with its grinning skull lying towards the east, lay a skeleton.

The Wildcat began to sweat. He counted a dozen skeletons and added a few dozen prayers to his perspiration. In a green alcove opening from the wider clearing seven skeletons stood erect in a ring about a flat stone.

His captors carried the Wildcat to this stone and held him. A little apart from him Running Bear opened the services with a yell which echoed like a chorus from the inferno.

The Wildcat gave up hope.

"They sho' got me. What dey is I don' know. Lemme go, boys."

The smoke from a dozen fires lifted in the clearing. Staggering in from half a dozen paths came as many painted warriors, each bearing on his back a salmon nearly as long as its red-skinned carrier.

Running Bear abandoned the vernacular for a moment and dropped into English.

"The Gods of the waters have sent the salmon. The black man can feast with his red brothers."

"Them words sure sounds noble. How come you pester me talkin' voodoo talk?"

"After the feast the fires of sacrifice will be lighted. It is written that one of our number shall be burned at the stake."

To the Wildcat's ears this sounded homelike, but not reassuring.

"Lemme go! Lemme go!"

He leaped from the rock and plunged through the fringing skeletons. Running Bear and a dozen of his companions loped along after the Wildcat. The galloping party covered the length of the island. Running Bear and his companions deployed in open order, to permit the Wildcat to double on his trail; but that panic-stricken individual had fixed his course, and he sailed true to it.

He headed for a twenty-foot bank, and his racing legs did not stop until the swirling waters of the Columbia had closed heavily over them.

Running Bear, who had followed as swiftly as his civilized muscles would permit, gazed anxiously at the swimming Wildcat for a moment, to reassure himself of his victim's safety.

"Go to it," he commented. "You'll make the mile in nothing flat with that panic crawl." He watched the Wildcat until the current swept him around the bend downstream.

"He's safe," Running Bear commented. "On with the dance."

He resumed the redskin role of a distant yesterday.

"Waugh!"

4.

In the gathering dusk the Wildcat swam and floated for a mile downstream in the currents of the Columbia; then under the insistent drag of a wide-swinging eddy he headed for the leading fences of a great salmon wheel whose plunging buckets dived into the black currents and lifted with their gamble of fifty-pound salmon. Now and then a heavier fish would punctuate the monotony of the catch.

Flopping among their more substantial companions a fleet of leaping steel heads added splashes of silver to the Chinook background.

The swimming Wildcat saw above him the descending framework of the fish wheel. He tried vainly to escape from the cage of wire netting falling from the sky upon him, but he was captured like a moth lost in a butterfly net.

"Lady Luck, good-bye."

The Wildcat dragged in a deep lungful of air as he went under. Five seconds later, preceded by three heavy-set salmon, he slithered down a trough into the storage bin in the hull of the fish wheel. About him were plunging fish. He looked at the square of evening light which glimmered through the hatch.

"Whah at is I?"

A fifty-pound salmon, sliding down the trough, struck fairly against the Wildcat's stomach.

"Fish, how come?"

Another leaping salmon slapped the Wildcat with his tail.

"Don't kick me wid yo' tail. I'll bust you in de haid."

The Wildcat struck wildly at the offending salmon. He slipped and fell into a vast fighting mass of lively fish. He wrestled with fins and tails.

He called loudly for Captain Jack and for Lady Luck. Once he thought his call was answered, but for half an hour the Wildcat led an unstable slippery life. He sought a bed of inert fish, only to awaken five or six gasping demons who flopped upon him heavily. He reached in vain for the hatch coaming five feet above him.

Half erect and with the deck timbers almost in his grasp, time and again his feet slipped from the back of a wriggling salmon.

"Dog-gone you, stand still; get pacified." He hauled off and slammed a kick at a salmon which had tripped him.

"I'll bust you in de belly."

He landed with his equator submerged by nine nervous fish. He sought to embrace a giant salmon. The Chinook slapped at him with his tail.

"Don' kick me wid yo' tail. I'll bust you in de nose."

He swung wildly at the salmon and was completely submerged. He came snorting to the surface of the mass.

"Whuff! Fish, git ca'm. Does yo' lay still I does."

5.

On deck near the hatch coaming in the early night Mr. Ogaloff Skooglund, the proprietor of the fish wheel, massaged his front teeth with Copenhagen snuff and figured his winnings.

"If de salmon fisk been running like dis tree day more Aye cleans oop sax t'ousand doller."

An echo from some unseen source seemed to reply.

Mr. Skooglund called loudly to the echo and then decided that he was crazy, for the call was repeated from the river bank.

The proprietor of the fish wheel yelled a greeting into the darkness.

Down the bank into the circle of light cast by a dim lantern came a fat man and a skinny individual with ears like a loving cup.

The fat man carried a wheat sack whose heavy contents jingled when he sat it on the deck of the fish wheel.

The pair were out of breath. The owner of the fish wheel stepped forward to try his English on his nocturnal visitors.

"Hello, fellers," he said.

The fat man answered, "Evenin'."

The skinny man tightened up on his ears for an instant and swung at Mr. Skooglund with a short club.

"Good evening," he said, accenting the blow. The Swede took the count with a grunt.

The fat man and the skinny one picked up Mr. Skooglund and carried him to the open hatch. Feet first they dropped him upon the slithering mass of salmon five feet below.

"He might drown. What did you hit him so hard for?"

"No chance. He ain't hurt--he'll sleep two or three hours. I only hit him light. You can't kill these fish fighters hittin' 'em in the head, anyway. Ivory--who's that?"

The fish wheel was being boarded by another visitor.

"Talk fish. You an' me owns the boat. We ain't seen nobody." The skinny man whispered quickly to his companion. "Kick that sack in the hold."

The wheat sack with its clinking contents was cast into the open hatch.

The Wildcat made another futile leap at the hatch coaming, just in time to catch the impact of the wheat sack and its jingling contents.

"How come?"

Then he twisted away from there and groaned a groan in which rumbled the anguished accents of horror. In the dim light he saw Mr.

Skooglund's face festooned completely by floundering salmon. Fear froze him.

"Salmon wid a man's face. I sho' is crazy."

Then to his ears from the deck of the fish wheel came the diverting tones of a voice which he had heard before. "The fat bad actor!"

"The fat bad actor!"

He listened for a moment to reassure himself, and then the motive of revenge was added to the other sources of inspiration which tensed the muscles of his legs. He leaped once more for the hatch coaming. This time he grabbed it. Silently he swung himself to the deck of the boat. Panting with his efforts, he lay quiet in the darkness.

In the dim lantern light he saw three figures.

The fat bad actor was speaking. "Naw, sir. Sheriff, we ain't seen nobody. We just bought this here wheel from the fellow that owned it yesterday. What did you say them train robbers looked like?"

The Wildcat snaked himself forward toward the fat bad actor. On the way his hand encountered the blade of an oaken oar. Thereafter for the next twenty feet he trailed the oar after him. He came within range and above the head of the fat bad actor lifted the heavy handle of the oar.

"Bam!"

On the instant the Sheriff leaped for the shadows. Out of the darkness came his voice.

"Don't move! Nobody!"

"Cap'n, I don' crave to move, an' de fat boy kain't, any more dan de dead man in de cellar."

The Sheriff's voice came out of the night clear as the cold stars. "Cut a piece of that rope and tie this man's hands."

The Wildcat was a little slow about tying a white man's hands, but he glanced at the blue-nosed equalizer dimly outlined in the Sheriff's steady hand and accelerated his gestures.

"Tie up that other man layin' on the deck. Tie them two men together."

"Cap'n, yessuh. How 'bout de dead boy layin' in de boat cellar?"

The Sheriff, fearing a ruse, hesitated for only a moment.

"Drop a rope down there and crawl down where he is. Tie it under his arms and then come back and haul him up."

"I's skeered to touch dat boy; feared he come back and follow me."

The Sheriff swung the gun at the Wildcat.

"Hurry up, before I spatter a hole through you."

"Cap'n, yessuh." The Wildcat made a line fast and threw the end of it into the hull of the fish wheel. He retrieved Mr. Skooglund from his environment of flopping salmon and tied the line under the arms of the inert man. He scrambled back on deck and hauled the Swede after him.

"Get a bucket of water and throw it on him."

Under this ungentle treatment the victim presently opened his eyes. He reached an unsteady hand to his head and inspected a knob thereon the size of an egg.

"Yust ven I hear de little angels iss singing, de earthquake troo de church down on me."

His vision encountered the Sheriff and the Wildcat.

"Was any salmon saved?"

The Sheriff reassured him.

"You had a wallop on the head. You're all right now." He abandoned Mr. Skooglund for a moment and turned to the Wildcat.

"Where's the dividend?"

"Cap'n, how come?"

"Come through with the clean up. You got enough watches and rings from them passengers to sink this craft."

"Mebbe it's de bag."

Convoyed by the swinging muzzle of the Sheriff's gun, the Wildcat dived again into the open hatch and returned presently with the jingling wheat sack swung about his shoulders.

The Sheriff inspected the contents.

"That's it."

He turned to the Swede.

"You able to walk?"

It seemed that Mr. Skooglund could navigate on his hind legs. The fat bad actor still lay unconscious on the deck. The Wildcat had done a good job with the oar, and it took six buckets of water to bring the fat man out of his slumbers. The quartette preceded the Sheriff down the narrow gang plank to the bank. They made their way a mile upstream and came upon the Sheriff's horse, hitched fast to a cottonwood on the river bank. The Sheriff fired his revolver three times in the air. Half an hour later he yelled loudly, and an answering call came from the distance through the night.

"That's the rest of the gang."

The party was joined presently by half a dozen riders. Two hours later the Wildcat, heavily ironed, rode beside Mr. Skooglund in the smoking car of the train headed for The Dalles. Dawn was breaking as the Sheriff and his companions marched up the street from the station.

Presently, in a cell apart from the rest of the world, the Wildcat heard the clanking of the heavy bolts which made the cell door a barrier.

"Lady Luck, how come?"

6.

Lady Luck was on the job. At eleven o'clock that morning the fat bad actor confessed, and in his confession the Wildcat was cleared.

A Deputy brought a telegram to the Sheriff. The Sheriff read it.

"Thousand dollars, hey? Looks to me like that nigger deserves the reward." The Sheriff was honest. "Fetch him in here."

The Wildcat was hazed into the Sheriff's presence.

"The railroad is paying a thousand dollars reward for roundin' up them two men. Maybe they'd got loose if you hadn't nailed that one in the head. I'll give you a letter to the Portland office and you can go down there and get your money."

"Cap'n, yessuh. Hot dam! Fish always was lucky with me."

Mr. Skooglund augmented the reward with a personal offer.

"Any time you wanting a salmon fisk I give you one free."

"Cap'n, suh, I sho' is much obliged, but if I neveh see a fish again, dat's twice too soon fo' me."

CHAPTER XI

The Wildcat felt noble. Against yesterday's clouds tomorrow's skies lay blue. The Sheriff's office at The Dalles was a comfortable place wherein to wait for the thousand-dollar reward which Lady Luck had showered down on her prodigal protege.

Half asleep, the Wildcat mumbled to a buzzing fly. "'At's it. Tryin' to bust yo' brains out on de window glass. 'At's how come you ain't got none. Cravin' to git loose all de time. S'pose you git loose? Whah at would you go? Some ol' spidah'd git you de fust mile. Ca'm yo'se'f. Heah you is in de sunshine an' all warmed up. You jess like folks--neveh knows when you's lucky."

The Wildcat's soliloquy was interrupted by a verbal volley from the Sheriff. "Here's your letter. Take it down to the railroad office in Portland; they'll pay you the thousand-dollar reward for helping capture that pair of train robbers."

"Cap'n, yessuh. Neveh seed so much money. Sho' come easy."

"Come easy, go easy. I suppose you'll load yourself up on square-face gin and get rolled the first night you're in town."

"No, suh, not me! I aims to 'vest mah money in de fried smelt business. Right now I's a Pullman porter. In Poteland mebbe I sees kin I buy myself free. Anyway, I starts me a smelt fish business. River's full ob ol' smelt fish. I ketches me a wagon load. I builds me a fire in mah fish wagon, an' when de fish is fried I sells 'em two bits a pan to de Poteland niggers. Neveh seed a nigger 'at wouldn't trade two bits fo' a belly full o' fish."

"Good-bye. Good luck with your smelt fish enterprise." The Sheriff terminated the interview.

The Wildcat stowed his thousand-dollar-reward letter in the inside pocket of the parade-leading Prince Albert which had seen temporary service as a Pullman porter's uniform.

He made his way to the railroad station and sat down at a point where a splash of sunlight dived into a pool of heat which radiated from the wall of the depot. For a little while his neck muscles held his head erect, and then, with his drooping eyelids, his head fell forward.

His meandering tongue offered an irresistible invitation to the mumbling fly which had escaped with the Wildcat from the Sheriff's office. The fly enjoyed the viscous environment until he succeeded in getting himself all squashed up in an instinctive gesture back of which were the clutching fingers of the Wildcat's swinging hand.

"Fly, how come you so confidential? 'At's mah pussonal tongue. On yo' way." The buzzer was batted into oblivion.

A moment later the roar of an incoming train sounded in the Wildcat's ears. "Fly sho' was handy. Sho' did me a good turn wakin' me up. Mebbe dey's got brains just like folks, else how come dey knows when it's train time?"

He boarded the train and settled down in a seat in the smoking car.

A Pullman porter from the twelve-wheeled battleship on the aft end of the train came forward and encountered the Wildcat. "Mawnin', boy; whah at you bound?"

"Poteland."

"You a Poteland boy?"

The Wildcat indulged in a little autobiography. "Not me. I 'filiates wid de Pullman company a long time back, conveyin' a westbound carload of Potent Nobles ob de Mystic Mecca wid blue Fezants. Us got divo'ced somewhere. Dey an' mah mascot goat gits drug to San F'mcisco. I gits penned up wid a rag-head Hindoo boy an' some crazy folks in anotheh train. I jines me in a ruckus wid train robbers. Den I busts loose, an' some Indian boys starts in to barbecue me. I swims myself free an' de ol' Sheriff gives me a thousan' dollahs fo' ketchin' 'em. Wish they'd been a dozen."

"Boy, I seed so many liars I got so I b'lieves lies, but yo' sho' strains me."

The Wildcat fished around in his parade-leading Prince Albert and produced the evidence. "Read dis letter. See does I strain you."

The infidel read the letter. He looked at the Wildcat. "Is yo' name Vitus Marsden?"

The Wildcat acknowledged his verbal label. "Folks gin'ally knows me as Wilecat, 'count o' me bein' de mil'tary Wilecat ob de Fust Service Battalion in France fo' so long."

The Pullman porter extended his hand. "Sho' glad to meet up wid you, Mistah Marsden. Mah name's Daniels. Dey gin'ally calls me Dwindle."

"Proud to meet you, Mistah Daniels. Did you come out ob de lion's den or de Navy?"

"Neither one. I'se a Bummin'ham Republican."

The Wildcat reached for his letter. "Gimme back dat letter. No boy f'm Alabam' is safe wid a money letter."

"How come?"

"Wust cleanin' I ever got in a' cube ruckus come off a Bummin'ham boy."

"Money come, money go. What you gonna' do when you gits yo' thousan' dollahs?"

"Fish business. I aims to start me a fried fish wagon in Poteland. Figgah out de profits. Heah's de ol' rivah dusty wid smelt fish. Heah's de Poteland niggahs cravin' to 'sorb fish mawnin', night, an' noon. I gits me some fryin' pans an' I cooks me up some fresh fish every day. Dey don't cost me nuthin'. I collects two bits a panful. 'At runs into big money."

Dwindle Daniels did some fast financial thinking.

"How does you aim to cook fish an' ketch 'em bofe, wid de Columbia river six miles f'm Poteland?"

The Wildcat hadn't thought of this detail. He made his associate a proposition.

"Dwindle, s'pose you 'filiates with me. Us ketches de fust wagon-load; den I fries fish an' collects de money whilst you ketches mo' fish."

"De fust day 'at's all right. Second day I's treasurer."

"Suits me."

For the next twenty miles the two fish financiers dived into the details of their commercial venture, and when the train slowed for the bridge leading across the Willamette to Union Station in Portland their plans were completed.

At the street gates of Union Station a policeman directed the Wildcat to the railroad offices. He lost the trail and wandered around for half an hour, but finally, with the assistance of a hundred questions, he made port.

An elevator boy directed him to the treasurer's offices, wherein presently he received a slip of blue paper in the lower right hand corner of which was the treasurer's signature.

"Cap'n, suh, what's dat?"

"That's a check for a thousand dollars."

"Dis papah?"

The Wildcat looked sideways at the check. "Whah at does I git de hard jinglin' money?"

"Any bank. Sign your name on the back of that check and any bank will cash it."

"Cap'n, suh, I ain't nevah learned to write. Kin you all help me wid dis papah?"

The clerk signed the Wildcat's name and underneath the signature the Wildcat made his mark.

"Stick here a minute and I'll get the money for you."

The clerk departed and returned presently with two thick packages of ten dollar bills.

"Money, howdy doo! 'At's more cash den I seed since payday in Bo'deaux."

Twenty minutes later the Wildcat languished in the lobby of a ramshackle hotel below Burnside Street, where he had a meeting date with his fish partner.

Dwindle Daniels at the moment was meshed in the net of official business.

To pass the time the Wildcat got fraternal with a languid brunet known as the Spindlin' Spider. The Spider's loose anatomy was draped with a complicated checked suit.

"Pardner, whah at kin a boy git a slug ob gin?"

"Cuba, mebbe. Gin comes high 'round heah, I knowed one drink to cost a boy ninety days."

"Ninety days, ninety dollars. Sometimes ol' square face gin sho' is worth it."

"Does yo' crave licker ten dollars' worth, sometimes dey's a white mule hitched in de back room."

The Wildcat pulled off a diplomatic boner. He displayed his thousand dollar roll and peeled therefrom a ten-dollar bill.

"Whah at kin I trade dis frog skin fo' a ra'r o' licker?"

Internally the Spindln' Spider suddenly awakened. He showed no outward sign of the agitation which the sight of the money had inspired, but for half an hour he played heavy politics, and thereafter, in a company of half a dozen hard-boiled crap shooters, the Wildcat began to pay for the indiscreet display of his cash.

"Leave dis Pullman boy take a r'ar at de clickers."

"'At's me. Hand me dem bones. C.O.D.--come on, dice! Field han's, rally round. Shoots fifty dollars. Shower down, brothers. Eagle bones, see kin you fly. Bam! I reads seven. I lets it lay. Shoots a hund'ed dollars! Fade me crazy, folks, fade me! Bam! I reads six--four. Slow death. Resurrection dice, an' I reads four--six."

The Wildcat hauled down part of his winnings.

"Shoots a hundred dollahs. Shower down, brothers. Spark in de powdeh! Both barrels. Right an' left. Bam! An' dey reads 'leven. Mowin' money. Us does a cash business. I lets it lay. Shower down yo' money!"

The Spindlin' Spider faced the Wildcat. "Boy, you donates."

"Don't sass me. Headed home wid feathers in yo' teeth. Telegraph dice, click fo' de coin. Bam!"

The Spider exercised his privilege of grabbing the dice before they had stopped rolling. As far as the Wildcat's naked eye could see, the same dice were rolled back at him, but as a matter of fact the Wildcat's dice nestled close against the epidermis of the Spindlin' Spider's right palm.

The dice that had been returned were festooned with misfortune. The Wildcat had overlooked a bet. He curried the gallopers to blood heat in his magenta palm. "Houn' dog headed home wid rabbit hair in yo' teeth! Turkey dice, gobble dat coin. Bam!--How come!"

An ace-deuce bloomed in the garden of chance.

The Spindlin' Spider faced the Wildcat. "Loses nuthin' but yo' money, boy. Roll 'em."

The Wildcat clipped his roll for another hundred. "Shoots a hund'ed. Shower down, fiel' han's! Dice hammer, drive de gold spike! Ten-o-see! An' I reads ace-dooce. How come I miss?"

The Spider repeated his comforting reminder: "Loses nuthin' but yo' money, brother. Roll 'em."

The Wildcat pared another stratum from his dwindling roll. "Shoots a hund'ed dollars. Grass cuttehs, reap dem greens! Fade me an' die poor. Bam! An' I reads--ace-dooce! Doggone, how come I set fire to de Chris'mus tree?"

"Ca'm yo'se'f." The Spindlin' brother dished out a little advice as he picked up his winnings. "What fo' you talk so much? You must think dis is a peace conflooence. Roll 'em."

Starting in the sunshine of Lady Luck's smile, the Wildcat cleared the hurdles of financial ruin and rambled into the stretch soggy with a cloudburst of hard luck. He staked his last pair of ten dollar bills on a throw whose momentum carried him to the cleaners.

The Spindlin' Spider urged him to lay further contributions on the altar of chance.

"I'se done. How come? Neveh seed such a hog for money. I'se cleaned now an' hung on de line. All I craves is five minutes wid Lady Luck, so I kin beat dat woman to death."

Thereafter for half an hour the Wildcat flopped dejected and inert in a chair in the lobby of the ramshackle hotel.

He tried vainly to borrow lunch money from the victorious Spindlin' Spider. "Ain't puttin' out nuthin' today." The Spider exhibited a heart of flint.

"Dem train robbehs sho' kain't learn yo' nuthin'." The Wildcat subsided in his chair. "Wish't ol' Cap'n Jack was here. Wish't dat doggone mascot goat hadn't lost me."

The lobby of the hotel was warm, and presently the pain of the Wildcat's financial bruises dissolved in the heated air. "Anyhow, I don't botheh work, work don't botheh me. I lost my money when de bones read three--

"I eats when I kin git it,
I sleeps mos' all de time.
I don' give a doggone
If de sun don't neveh shine."

The Wildcat's head dropped forward, and presently he was doing the best he could to sleep for ever.

CHAPTER XII

The Wildcat's siesta was interrupted by a rumbling voice which emanated from a chesty policeman who was engaged in dishing out a little earnest advice to the proprietor of the hotel. The officer raised his voice for the benefit of the brunet assemblage.

"Trouble is trouble. If yez have business on th' street, attind to ut, but save th' loafin' f'r another day. Wid all thim I.W.W. bugs, this nigrah parade tonight is apt to flash into a race riot. If it does, th' chief ain't goin' to stan' no foolin'. The guns'll begin barkin' worse than a Chinee New Year. Don't look for no trouble an' you won't find it. You boys ain't much in favour in this town right now, an' wan false move in tonight's parade might make a stampede out of it, wid all th' dark complexions in town three jumps ahead of some red-hot buckshot."

The Wildcat shrivelled up in his chair. The policeman's warning made him homesick. He resolved to stick close to the home plate. "Ah don't crave no paradin' roun' whah at white folks is. Dese uppity yaller niggahs sho' heads fo' trouble when dey starts speakin' white folks' talk. Wish't ol' Cap'n Jack was here. He'd sho' learn 'em, did dey start sumpin'. Like as not ol' Cap'n Jack tear down a lamp post an' beat de parade ovah de head wid it. Parades is all right fo' crematizin' ceremonies. All right fo' de Ahmy boys. All right fo' funerals an' lodges. Outside o' dat dey's dangerous. Me, Ah sees kin I sleep me some mo'."

His slumbers were again interrupted by the entrance of the porter whose acquaintance he had made en route from The Dalles to Portland.

"Boy, howdy."

The Wildcat sat up and blinked a pair of heavy lids over his bulging eyes. "Doggone if it ain't mah ol' fish podneh. Sho's glad to meet up wid you. How is you?"

"Tol'able, 'ceptin' I's rushed. Us got to work dis fish business fast. I don't git me no lay-over. Ol' Pullman boy's done switched me to de midnight run fo' San F'mcisco on de train what leaves at one o'clock in de mawnin'. Dat's why I ain't change' my unifawm. How is you? Did de man give you de money fo' de train robbeh letter?"

The Wildcat's face, which had lightened in greeting his partner in the smelt fish business, was suddenly overspread with a mask of melancholy. "Easy come, easy go. I's busted."

"How come you bust now, when dis mawnin' yo' back was broke wid a thousand-dollah letter?"

"Met up wid a Spindlin' boy what hit me wid some C.O.D. dice. Cleaned me."

"Sho' ha'd luck. You sho' got action. Neveh min', I'se got 'nuff to start de fish business wid. Dey's a parade tonight, and us cleans up big, sellin' fish to de parade niggers."

The pair launched into the working details of their fried fish business.

"Wilecat, I got me some rubbah boots. Us hires a wagon and rambles over to de C'lumbia River. We loads up on smelt fish an' rambles back. We fries de fish in de back end ob ol' wagon on a oil stove."

"Whah at's de oil stove? Whah at's de wagon?"

"Us rents de wagon from a livery stable boy I knows, fo' four bits. I knows where us kin git a oil stove f'm a boy on Front Street. Temporary, that is. Oil stoves comes high now."

"Le's go."

"Wait 'til I gits my rubbah boots."

The porter reappeared from his room wearing a pair of knee-length rubber boots.

"Sho' is de biggest boots I ever seed," the Wildcat commented.

The Wildcat held the door open until his companion had navigated the channel with the brace of ponderous violins which festooned his feet and trotted along towards the livery stable in cadence with the tromping extremities of Dwindle Daniels.

"Sho' is de biggest foot caves I ever seed. Was you in de army yo' could come from parade rest to 'tenshun without movin' dem boots."

At the livery stable Dwindle Daniels financed the rental of a light wagon and a heavy-set mule. The Wildcat gathered up the reins. "Set down fo' I starts," he advised. "Kain't tell about dese jug-heads."

The pair discovered presently that the mule's maker had omitted the high gear from the animal's mechanism, and the six-mile trip was accomplished at a four-mile gait. The mule was equally indifferent to leather and language. "'Spec' mebbe he's delicate. Some is. Comin' back I gits me a saplin' an' sees is he. No mule neveh konkered me yit."

They arrived presently at the bank of the fish-crowded Columbia River, where the business of loading their wagon with smelt occupied them for less than an hour.

"Neveh seed so many fish. Ol' river sho' is dusty wid fish. Did dese fish have laigs a boy couldn' git down de road past 'em."

With the work of the moment completed, Dwindle Daniels obeyed some instinct of neatness. He threaded his way out along an overhanging piece of driftwood to the clear water of the river, wherein he proposed to wash his hands.

The Wildcat watched him for a while and then broke into criticism. "How come yo' so neat? Yo' acts like a barber shop boy, all de time cleanin' up. Next thing you'll be cravin' bear grease fo' yo' hair an' a sprinkle o' bay rum."

"I craves to smell human," the porter returned. "All right fo' fish to smell like fish, but I prefers to let 'em win any smell race dey starts."

In replying to the Wildcat, Dwindle Daniels on his slippery perch half turned his head, and this carelessness precipitated a disaster which engulfed him. One of the ponderous boots slipped from the branch of driftwood and dragged the wearer's leg into the river. Thereafter for ten seconds the porter staged a windmill scene compared to which a cyclone in Holland looked like a quiet night on the Dead Sea. Finally the drag of old man Gravity won all bets. The Wildcat's bulging eyes witnessed a high dive entirely surrounded by frightened fish and the soft mud which lay two feet below the water surface. From the crater of the mud volcano the writhing form of the neat Dwindle Daniels finally emerged. His form-fitting environment of mud churned and splashed in a blast of agitated language. Somewhere in the vortex of the intimate ooze he had lost all traces of his religious training. He combed great handfuls of mud from his plastered features and snorted deep draughts of fresh air.

He excavated his eyes and then, disdaining the unstable footing offered by the driftwood, he ploughed his way ashore, up to his arm pits in water and mud.

On the bank the Wildcat had launched into his third conniption fit. He calmed down sufficiently to choke some language out of his vocal organs.

"Yo' sho' looks neat now. Ain't seed such a ruckus since de flood hit

Memphis. I knowed dem was hoodoo boots. Bam! Down yo' goes like a ol' hell diver. Mawnin'! Up yo' comes like a ol' mud turtle. Git in de wagon, Mud Turtle. On de way home you dries out. Leave dat mud git dry befo' you tries to brush it off."

Dwindle Daniels spent an hour on the way home in hatching himself out of a shell of mud.

"Neveh min', ol' Mud Turtle," the Wildcat comforted. "Us cleans up big money when us sells dese fish tonight."

At eight o'clock, under a sputtering arc light on Front Street, the Wildcat and Dwindle Daniels were established in the business of selling fried fish and waiting for the rush of trade that would come when the parade passed them.

"Stan' close to de oil stove, ol' Mud Turtle. I cracks de shell off o' you befo' de train leaves. Dis sho' is de slow dryenest mud I ever seed. Leave them pants on you. Does you take 'em off you neveh gits 'em back. Stan' still."

The Wildcat broke a few pounds of mud from the porter's uniform.

"Stan' close to de blaze. When de mud dries you peels easy as a shell-bark hick'ry nut."

The success of the peeling process was all gummed up at nine o'clock by the Portland humidity, which won its usual bet. From the heavy skies a light rain began to fall.

At half past nine, with the booming drums of the parade sounding up the street, the shivering form of Dwindle Daniels was again sogged down to its original saturation point.

"Wilecat, I don' see how kin I make mah run to San F'mcisco."

"Yo' makes yo' run all right. Yo' dead-heads me, an' I does yo' work whilst yo' hangs out de front vegetable ob de car. Ol' wind dry yo' out sudden. Git ready fo' de gran' rush. Here's de head ob de parade."

The Wildcat threw back his head and bawled into the evening air: "Fried fish! Smelt fish! Here you is, two bits a pan!"

He lowered his head to gratify his curiosity concerning the technique of beating a bass drum. "Sho' craves 'at boy's job. Some day when I gits rich I buys me a bass drum. 'At drum bammer sho' swings a mean club."

"Fried fish! Smelt fishes! Two bits a pan!"

Following the band and leading the parade, heavily laden with a false dignity which had completely eradicated his spinal curvature, there appeared the rag-head Hindoo who had escaped with the Wildcat from the carload of undesirable aliens on the night of the train robbers' fiesta below The Dalles.

A little before the head of the parade reached the arc light under which the Wildcat and Dwindle Daniels had inaugurated their fish business, the Hindoo turned and raised his arms.

The parade stopped.

The rag-head signalled for his companions to come close about him.

In precise English he broke into a violent harangue wherein the least radical of the evil doctrines which he preached would have been sufficient to transform the United States into a second Russia.

Midway of his speech one of the accompanying platoon of police officers stepped up to him.

"Can that stuff, you Anarchist! Come wid me!"

The officer reached for the Hindoo, and this gesture of the law's hand was a signal which launched a riot into being.

"Boy, dis looks like a bad ruckus!" The Wildcat spoke quickly to Dwindle Daniels. "Wish't ol' Cap'n Jack was here. Chances is, us niggahs gits lynched."

On the tense instant of conflict a solution to the threatening disaster was born to the Wildcat. With all the energy of his lungs, he bawled his peace message into the turmoil of the night.

"Free fish! Hot fish free! Come an' git it!"

Fifty feet from him the rag-head Hindoo broke loose from the police officer. The Wildcat witnessed the escape. The Hindoo raced towards him, and it was then that mutual recognition was accomplished. The Wildcat leaped into the fugitive's pathway and extended his foot.

The Hindoo Anarchist pulled a galloping somersault. He revolved twice in the air, and then his face ploughed heavily into the pavement.

"Hot dam! Neveh seed a boy so agile!"

The police officer exercised the good judgment common to the majesty of the law in moments of great mental stress.

He made a swing at the Wildcat with his stick.

"Plunk!"

The locust club impacted heavily on the Wildcat's skull.

The Wildcat blinked his eyes. "How come? Cap'n, suh, I thought yo' craved to ketch dat rag-head boy!"

He pointed at the inert Hindoo lying on the pavement.

"Didn't aim to hit you."

"Cap'n, yes, suh." The Wildcat hoped that the next time the policeman would aim straight at him. He turned to the crowd and renewed his pacifying propaganda.

"Free fish! Come an' git it. Here you is, boys!"

The Wildcat's invitation and the smell of the frying smelt won the field against the doctrines of the defeated agitator. A minute later the fish wagon was ringed about with a hundred brunet fish eaters. The riot had evaporated. Here was the end of the trail.

Serious thinking gave place to heavy eating. Crazy ideas no longer tormented heads whose owners' object in life was to eat more fried smelt than the men next to them.

The sergeant commanding the platoon of police sized up the situation. "Looks to me like the end of a perfect day."

A brother officer addressed the sergeant. "Better take this rag-head in with us. How about it?"

"Sure. Book him as a vag until we see who he is. Tell Jimmy to hold him on an A and B charge if any of them jail-breaking law sharks try to spring him."

The Wildcat broke in with a little testimony.

"Cap'n, suh, I knows dat boy. He bust loose from a travellin' jail on de train comin' from Chicago. The guv'ment men ketched him some place."

The sergeant of police looked quickly at the officer whose fingers were closed about the chain attached to the handcuffs of the Hindoo's wrists.

"Hear what this boy says? Maybe this rag-head is that agitatin' alien that got loose from the carload that landed here three days ago."

"How about holdin' this fellow for a witness?" The officer nodded his head towards the Wildcat. The Sergeant debated for a moment, during which the Wildcat's freedom wavered in an unstable balance.

Finally the Sergeant spoke, and with his words the Wildcat's liberty was assured. "We don't need him. We've got enough to hold this rag-head with--and the bull pen is crowded anyhow."

The Wildcat got the drift of the crisis which had passed. "Cap'n, suh, I sho' is obliged to you. Me an' ol' Mud Turtle here aims to take our midnight run to San F'mcisco."

The Mud Turtle, who was busy dealing out free fried smelt, paused long enough to crack a few segments of dried mud from his uniform. He hit himself on the chest, and another nickel-plated button in an area of blue cloth was revealed in the light of the street lamp.

"Us sho' do," he confirmed. "Me an' dis Wilecat boy's Pullman men."

A few minutes later the Wildcat augmented the disappearing supply of free fish with a little sound advice to his patrons.

"Neveh seed such fool niggers. Was ol' Cap'n Jack here he sho' would ca'm you down wid a club. You gits yo' haids full ob crazy notions, an' after de ruckus dey hauls you out feet fust. Think like white folks does if you craves to, but unless you aims to festoon yo' health an' strength wid a funeral box an' lead a graveyard procession, stop wid de thinkin'. Think like white folks does, but don't act dat way. Next time, befo' you 'filiates wid any wild men, say howdy to a mess o' vittles. De river's full o' free fish, an' de jail's full o' crazy folks like dat rag-head Hindoo boy. Next time anybody tells you you's de same as white folks, bust him in de nose an' walk away fast. 'At's all."

The Wildcat ended his preaching and turned to his associate.

"Come on heah, ol' Mud Turtle. Le's take dis mule an' wagon back to dat liv'ry stable boy befo' us gits 'rested fo' lendin' him permanent."

CHAPTER XIII

The Wildcat drove to the livery stable. The Mud Turtle, seated beside him, spent the time en route to the place in scraping the mud from his southern hemisphere.

At the livery stable he removed his ponderous rubber boots and sloshed his feet with a hose. He paid the rent for the mule and wagon. "Heah's fo' bits mo'. Take dat oil stove back to dat sto' by de riveh," he directed.

Carrying the boots in his hand, he walked beside the Wildcat toward the ramshackle hotel below Burnside Street.

In the cold night a summary of the day's misfortunes settled heavily on the marching pair. "Sho' turned out rough," the Mud Turtle remarked.

The Wildcat sought a smile in the frown which had gathered on Lady Luck's features.

"Sho' might been worse. S'posin' you'd been drowned in de riveh. S'posin' dat policeman had took me to jail. S'posin' I'd a had two thousan' dollars 'stid o' one when 'at boy cleaned me. Naw, suh! Us is half lucky. Wish't I could meet up wid 'at boy now an' give him a ride wid a pair o' taper bones like de Backslid Baptis' used to make."

The Mud Turtle looked sideways at the Wildcat. "Boy, you an' me is podnehs. Confidential, I tells you does you crave taper bones I has me a pair."

"Is you? Lemme see, Mud Turtle, lemme see!"

The porter fished around in an inside pocket of his soggy uniform and produced a pair of green dice.

"Heah dey is. I dassn't use 'em. Ain't learned de thumb twist yit, an' dey sho' means trouble is you ketched workin' 'em."

"Gimme dem bones, boy. I craves trouble wid dat Spindlin' niggah what cleaned me. Gimme ten dollahs. Pray to Lady Luck to have dat boy waitin' at de hotel. By rights 'at's my money. Does I meet up wid dat boy I sho' cleans him rough!"

The Mud Turtle handed the dice and ten-dollar bill to the Wildcat. "Lady Luck don't have to do nuthin'. That boy nevah is anywhere else 'cept at de hotel. Does you start sumpin' finish quick! It's midnight now, an' 'at San F'mcisco train pulls out at one o'clock."

The Wildcat paid no heed to his companion's words. He was engaged in twisting the dice in the nervous fingers of his right hand.

"Dey feels right! Dey sho' feels right! Boy, de thumb twist come to me befo' I was nine yeahs old. When I was fo'teen mah uncle Gabe learnt me neveh to dooce, trey, or twelve. Wid dese bones an' yo' ten-dollah bill, when I gits th'oo wid 'at nigger he won't have no mo' money than a frog has feathers."

The pair entered the hotel.

The Mud Turtle went directly to his room, wherein he began the difficult business of oozing his number twelve feet into a pair of number ten shoes.

The Wildcat sought the Spindlin' Spider in whose web he had sacrificed his thousand dollars earlier in the day.

He found his man leaning against a pool table in a room adjoining the lobby of the hotel.

"Howdy, boy." The honeyed accents of gentle forgiveness dripped from the Wildcat's quiet salutation.

The Spindlin' Spider looked at him. "Howdy. How is you?"

"Me? I's noble--an' bustin' wid a cravin' fo' revenge." The Wildcat raised his voice. "Shoots ten dollahs!"

Under the flat nose of the Spindlin' Spider he waved the ten-dollar bill which he had borrowed from the Mud Turtle.

The Spider produced a roll of bills and peeled a ten spot therefrom. "Roll 'em! You an' me both craves action."

The Wildcat had hooked his fish.

He twisted the green taper dice in a handful of fingers whose tips bulged with a fine technique that had distilled from years of study and practice.

Here on the green cloth of the pool table was his field of battle.

Before him lay his entire capital, matched by an equal amount from the Spindlin' Spider's roll.

"I's a Wildcat for revenge, an' I's on my prowl! Pay-day dice, speak mah name! Bam! Five and a dooce. I lets it lay. Shower down!"

The Spindlin' Spider covered his bet.

"Gallopers, stay lame on seven. Train robber babies, fo'ty dollars in de sack. I reads six-five! Rally roun', boys. Shoots fo'ty dollars. Fade me, boy. Bugle dice, blow de cash call. Harvest babies, pick yo' cotton! Bam! An' I reads fo' trey!"

The Wildcat stowed away a trio of ten-dollar bills as an insurance policy against accident.

"Shoots fifty dollars!"

The Spindlin' Spider shaved five ten-dollar bills from his roll, "Roll 'em," he said.

The Wildcat lifted his brace of tapered cubes high above his head.

"Honey-bee babies, git yo' stinger hot. Shotgun dice, spout yo' lead. Key cubes, unlock de han'cuffs. Bam! Dey reads seven. I lets it lay. Shower down, boy. Fade me. Shoots a hund'ed dollars!"

"You're faded." The Spider had his feet wet, and now he waded deeper into the river of revenge.

The Wildcat rolled the dice against his legs.

"Squirrel dice, ketch de top limb! Ham cubes, drip yo' gravy! Mule bones, resurrection morn. Breakin' on de B. & O.--Bust an' out. Baptisin' babies, hold his head under."

The gallopers rattled across the pool table and went to sleep with a six-five staring the Spindlin' Spider in the face.

"I lets it lay! Shoots two hundred dollars. De gin dice makes de big boy sick. Fade me, ol' mule-lip. What fo' is yo' mouth draggin'?"

A look of doubt began to travel across the Spindlin' Spider's features, but the moral pressure of the crowd about him forced him into the slaughter house. He counted two hundred dollars from his roll and laid it beside the Wildcat's stake.

The Wildcat breathed the hot breath of hope upon the twin cubes in his hand. "Lady dice, git lovely. Snake babies, coil 'roun' de coin. Grub cubes, 'semble yo' rations! Army gallopers, as you was! Bam!"

The green clickers subsided near the end cushion of the pool table. A five spot smiled on the top side of one and a helpful dooce laughed cheerfully at the Wildcat from the other.

"Hot dam! Weddin' dice done rung de bell. 'At's fo' hund'ed dollars. Shoots fo' hundred! Fade me! You says yo' blood is hot fo' action. Fade me!"

The lower jaw swinging from the Spindlin' Spider's face drooped something less than a foot. His expression was suddenly full of quinine. He craved an exit while the exit business was good, but a reputation created by considerable indiscreet language had locked the door.

From his depleted roll he laid down forty ten-dollar bills.

"'At about cleans me." He looked at the remains of his stake. "'At about cleans me."

His voice had lost the aggressive quality which had marked his oratory five minutes earlier.

"'At's eight hund'ed dollars. More like I's used to shootin'." The Wildcat rubbed his fingers' tips quickly across the taper cubes.

"Eight hund'ed iron men. Lady Luck, stan' by me! Preacheh bones, make 'em bow down. Riveh dice, high an' dry. Over de riffle. Whuff! Bam! An' I reads seven."

"Ump!" The Spindlin' Spider grunted an accompaniment to a wave of grey which lightened the ebony of his features.

The Wildcat picked up the mass of banknotes and straightened them out. He turned to the Spider. "Mule Lip, how much is you got left? Shoots you fo' what you's got. Mebbe you builds up. Neveh can tell. Mah luck's boun' to break sometime."

The Spider replied weakly, "I'se got mine. 'At's plenty."

"What you mean you's got yours? Thought you claimed you was a spo't. You's got money, ain't you? You ain't got yours till you goes broke. Ain't I right, boys?"

The Wildcat made a quick survey of the faces about him.

From the lips of the Mud Turtle, who had silently joined the group, came a come-on verdict. "You sho' is."

"Hear dat?" The Wildcat turned again to the Spindlin' Spider. "Hear dat? You ain't got yours till you goes broke. How much is you got? Shoots it all. Double or nuthin'."

The Spider weakly disgorged his roll. He counted out a total of two hundred dollars.

"Boy--one pass an' I cleans you. Li'l snow flakes, sof'ly fall. Come on, dice, C.O.D.--Bam! An' de black specs read--seven. Hot dam! Boy, you's done. Lady Luck, heah you is!"

The Wildcat pocketed his roll of bills and covered the money with a wide palm wherein lay the taper cubes. He edged through the crowd. With his left hand he reached for the Mud Turtle.

"Come on heah, boy. Dat San F'mcisco train gits nervous doggone soon."

In the vestibule of the Mud Turtle's car on the San Francisco train the Wildcat held out the taper cubes and a handful of winnings. "Ol' Mud Turtle, heah's yo' victory dice an' fo' hund'ed dollars. Dat gits you a new unifawm. Git in dere by de steampipes whilst I tells dem passenger folks where de San F'mcisco train goes to. Hot dam! I knowed dem smelt fish was lucky!"

The Mud Turtle pocketed his dice. "Wilecat, I's lucky too. Fall in de riveh an' comes out wid fo' hund'ed dollahs! You sho' got speed!"

"Call dat speed--wait till us 'cumulates mah mascot goat. Den us heats up dem C.O.D. dice, an' Ah shows you what me an' Lady Luck kin do when de speed bell rings. You ain't seed no speed yet!"

CHAPTER XIV

Leaving Portland an hour after midnight, the deadhead Wildcat sat in the smoking room of the Mud Turtle's San Francisco bound Pullman. The Passengers were in bed. On the window end of the leather seat, shivering himself out of a coating of Columbia river mud which he had accumulated that afternoon during the smelt harvest, was the Mud Turtle.

"Boy, dem shivers is workin' overtime. Neveh seed such a partial-shiverin' fool. How come yo' mis'ry gits you by fractions? Shiver all over an' git done wid it. Is you cold inside?"

The Mud Turtle forcibly arrested his chattering teeth. He calmed his
vocal organs and answered the Wildcat, but when he became articulate
his feet assumed the staccato movement.

The Wildcat looked at him. "Stan' up befo' you loses dat step. Leave me
learn 'at new foot work. I nevah seed feet so anxious. Don't waste dem
steps." The Mud Turtle grabbed his knees and shoved his feet firmly
against the floor of the car. "Wilecat, what I needs is gin till I gits
warmed up."

"You an' me bofe. Any boy needs gin. I been needin' it since away back.
You sho' looks cold. Was you a' ice man you'd be rich. I'se seed folks
cold an' I'se seed 'em shiver, but it sho' looks to me, Mud Turtle,
like you'se de champion shimmy king ob de worl'. Ketch dat leg!
Doggone, boy, you sho' would be pop'lar durin' de hot spell down where
us comes f'um. You makes me cold lookin' at you."

The Mud Turtle's jaws started on another chattering ruckus.

"Dere you goes agin! Now you cain't talk. Whilst you'se dumb I'se a
mind to use some cuss words on you what ol' Cap'n Jack learned me. Sho'
would use 'em, 'ceptin' dey'd burn you to a cinder. Stay here whilst I
'vestigates an' sees kin I 'cumulate some stove juice to heat you up
wid."

The Wildcat walked ahead through the train. He sought strong drink from
every porter he encountered, but his search was unsuccessful until he
came to the dining car.

"Whah at you think you is? Heavin? Cuba? Ain't nuthin' to drink on dis
car." A burly chef answered the Wildcat's inquiry.

"Dey's a cold boy back dere. Fell in de river an' stood out in de night rain in Poteland. Can't git near him for' chips o' teeth flyin' through de air. When he gits to shiverin' good he looks like him an' two twin brothehs."

"White boy?" The chef ventured a casual inquiry.

"Is I said white boy? White boy packs it wid 'em. It's mah ol' Mud Turtle podneh what craves de gin."

"'At's diff'unt." The chef grunted and got up from the poker game which was raging. "Come wid me." He led the Wildcat into the kitchen of the car. From one of the cupboards against the partition he lifted a pint bottle full of a light yellow fluid. He poured some of this into a smaller bottle. Out of another bottle containing a brown aromatic liquid he filled the third bottle. He shook the smaller bottle until the two liquids in it were mixed. He handed the bottle to the Wildcat. "Give dat boy dis."

"Sho' will. What's de name o' dis licker?"

"Ain't got no public name. Us boys calls it 'hoof oil.' It kicks--some. Better tie 'at boy's hind laigs does he take mo'n two drinks."

"What's de 'mgredients?"

"Dat's a church secret. Don't ask me no questions. 'At's five dollahs."

"Five dollahs! What you mean church secret?"

"I'se a hooch rabbi, off de run. I leads a Oakland ginagogue. I said five dollahs. How you spec' us rabbis gwine to thrive, 'ceptin' by takin' up de collection now an' den when we issues dis here rabbi juice?"

"How come dat rabbi name?"

The chef looked at him. "You sho' is a' ignorant niggah. Ain't you met up wid no rabbis yet?"

"Cain't say I is. What is dey?"

In the chef's gaze was an expression of contempt. "Boy, when you sees me you sees a rabbi. I works at de rabbi business between trips. De rabbi lodge was o'ganized wid all de culled bartenders. Now days mos' all we rabbis is union bootleggers. Git back dah wid dat hoof oil befo' it blows up. Whereat's de five dollahs?"

The Wildcat handed the chef a five-dollar bill and returned to his car, where the Mud Turtle was doing the best he could to shake his arms off.

"Hot dam! Heah you is, ol' Mud Turtle. You sho' got a noble rattle in yo' right han'. 'Pears like wid a pair o' gallopin' cubes you might throw some killin' sevens. 'Sorb one drink o' dis heah rabbi juice an' resurrect yo'self."

"One drink! Boy, gimme dat bottle. I handles mah licker!" The Wildcat uncorked the bottle and held it to the Mud Turtle's chattering lips. The Mud Turtle took a whiff of the liquid. Its perfume seemed to inspire a new set of internal calisthenics in the Mud Turtle. After he had quit writhing the Wildcat again pressed the remedy upon him. "Drink it, fo' I drips it on you. Go ahead an' drink. I'll hol' yo' nose." He succeeded in pouring the contents of the bottle into the Mud Turtle.

The Mud Turtle absorbed the hoof oil as far as his equator. Then he reacted with a series of undulations in which was all of the reserve energy of the surging deep. Then he suddenly became quiet, except for his rolling eyeballs, from which gleamed an exalted light.

"Dat sho' tamed you. Is yo' insides hot?"

The Mud Turtle's only reply was a sudden stiffening of his right leg, followed a second later by a similar movement with his left. His right arm extended violently; then the ham-sized fist on the end of his left arm went through the plate glass window beside him. He leaped to the centre of the smoking compartment. For a moment he danced on both feet, and then he began to stage a movement compared to which a cyclone was only a boy's-size disturbance. He combined the activity of a whirling dervish with the technique of an earthquake.

The Wildcat retreated to the safety of the tapestry curtain which hung in the doorway. There for a little while he conducted an innocent bystander business, which presently ended in disaster. Up to the moment, the Mud Turtle had been silent, but now from his throat came a yelp which drowned the rattle of the train.

The Wildcat sought to calm him down. "How come? Boy, git tame. You'll wake de white folks in dis car an' dey'll massacre you. Shut up befo' dey gits you."

The Mud Turtle's only answer was a renewed succession of yells. Suddenly he stopped short where he stood, and for a space of minutes he regarded his companion with a pair of glassy eyes under whose hypnotic spell the Wildcat began to shrivel.

"Don' look dat way. You's got de graveyard eye. You took too much hoof oil," he said weakly. "Lemme put 'at blanket 'roun' you." He took one step towards the centre of the compartment, and on the instant the Mud Turtle leaped at him.

The Wildcat had been in many a ruckus abroad and at home, but home was never like this, and the worst he saw in France was a busy time at Chateau Thierry. This was different trouble and worse. The Wildcat abandoned his tactics of fair fighting. He kicked and struck wildly at the Mud Turtle without effect. He despaired of conquering the tornado which writhed on the floor beside him. Then he succeeded in obtaining the blanket in which the Mud Turtle had been wrapped. He manoeuvered for three seconds and threw a hitch around the Mud Turtle's neck and another one around his leg. An instant later the whirlwind was trussed up and confined with a hard square knot.

The Mud Turtle's yells gave place to a series of snarling grunts, punctuated now and then with the yowling scream invented some years back by the female panther. The Wildcat secured a folded towel from the rack above his head, and in a moment the panther was muffled. The victor stood panting for a little while, gazing at the conquest which still writhed and rolled on the floor.

The Wildcat reached for the empty bottle and inspected five or six drops of liquid which remained in it. "Hoof oil, you sho' is double dynamite. Rabbi juice, I saves you. Mebbe sometime I meets up wid a army whut starts a ruckus wid me. Den I'll 'sorb two drops an' win de battle."

He replaced the cork in the bottle and stowed it carefully in his pocket. "Does I need to I figger dat wid fo' drops ob dis hoof oil I kin conquer de worl'."

He turned again to the Mud Turtle. The Pullman blanket lashed around the Mud Turtle cramped his style to a considerable degree, but for all of his impedimenta he was still active enough to threaten the peace-on-earth theory. The Wildcat spoke to him, "Boy, I sequesters you till de debbil leaves you. Mebbe by de time us gits to San F'mcisco you'll be human again."

He stepped into the passage way, and at the end of the open section of the car he opened the door of the linen closet. He returned to the smoking room and dragged the Mud Turtle out of the room wherein the ruckus had been staged. At the door of the linen closet the Wildcat encountered a difficult problem, in that the least dimension of the Mud Turtle in his present pose was greater than the width of the door.

He grabbed the door framing with both hands and applied his right foot to the Mud Turtle's anatomy. "Whuf! Git in dere!" He strained hard at his task, and presently a heroic effort was rewarded by the disappearance of the Mud Turtle into the dark interior of the linen closet. The Wildcat stooped down and removed the towel from about the Mud Turtle's mouth. "Yell yo' head off, ol' debbil. You kain't soun' loud in heah. Folks'll think de ol' engine is whistlin'."

Before the Wildcat shut the door the Mud Turtle took advantage of his vocal freedom and emitted a strenuous howl. A middle-aged gentleman half way down the car stuck his head through the berth curtains. He called to the Wildcat. "Is she whistlin' for Ashland?"

"No suh. 'Spec' it was a cow on de track or sumpin'. 'At's all. I wakes you up neah Ashlan'." The Wildcat neglected to say which side of Ashland would be selected for the awakening ceremonies.

He walked to the far end of the car, and on his return journey he accumulated the shoes of his passengers.

"I shines me dese heah shoes an' den I sees kin I sleep me some. I bet was ol' Mud Turtle a aig, chances is he'd hatch out in dat linen closet--so hot."

In the smoking compartment the Wildcat spent an hour shining shoes. He distributed them with more or less accuracy, and presently he was stretched out sound asleep on the long leather seat.

"I eats when I kin git it,
I sleeps mos' all de time.
I don't give a doggone
If the sun don't neveh shine."

CHAPTER XV

The Wildcat slept until the first grey light of dawn announced the day. He got up and stretched himself and drank five or six slugs of free ice water. "Lemme see," he yawned, "whah at is us." His mind covered the events of his immediate past and collided heavily with the battle which had been fought in the night. "Wondeh how ol' Mud Turtle is? I betteh git him fo' de passengers gets up. Wid all dat hoof oil in 'im, 'spec' he'll crave mo' wateh dan a mule."

He opened the door of the linen closet. In the far corner, propped against the wall, sat the Mud Turtle. The dazed expression on his face was completely surrounded by brunet skin and surmounted by a pair of owl-like eyes which blinked at the sudden light.

The Wildcat whispered at him, "Is you pacified? Dast I leave you loose?"

The Mud Turtle replied with a question, "Was many folks hurt in de wreck?"

"Ain't been no wreck, 'ceptin' you like to wrecked me. Come out heah till I helps you 'membeh yo' sinful past."

He hauled the Mud Turtle into the passage way and resurrected him from the interior of the blanket cocoon.

"Come on back heah," the Wildcat directed. "Stretch yo' laigs an' come on back heah whilst I 'splains about you. Take 'at ol' coat off an' put on dis white coat."

The Mud Turtle removed his mud-caked blue coat and donned a crisp white jacket. For a while he sat quiet on the leather seat of the smoking car. Finally he turned to the Wildcat.

"All I 'members is takin' one drink."

"All I 'members pusson'ly is what you did after you took 'at one drink. Thought you said you could handle yo' licker. I neveh seed such a wild man. Boy, you started single, but when you an' 'at drink got confidential you sho' was a' army. Handle yo' licker! Huh! You couldn' handle de bottle, let alone what was in it. How come you lie such a big lie? Start out gentle nex' time."

"Must a bin some new kin' o' licker."

"Sho' acted new. Wid one drink like dat in me when I was fightin' in France, de ole guv'ment wouldn't need no mo' soldiers. I seed de night ob de big wind what blowed New Awl'uns clean up de Mississippi River. I know'd a mule what couldn't live in de mountains 'count o' kickin' 'em over, but las' night when you was goin' good, I says, 'If a mule married a cyclone an' had a boy, he'd be you.' 'Hoof oil,' dey calls it. 'At niggah what chefs in de dinin' car an rabbis when he lays over in Oaklan' give it to me."

The Mud Turtle looked at the broken window beside him. "Did I bus' 'at window?"

"Bust 'at window--you sho' did. All you did was blow yo' breaf at it. I tell you you was bad. I's seed folks what was plastered wid luck. You thinks you's plastered wid mud, but it ain't mud; it's real ol' luck. You had all de luck in de worl' gettin' out ob de claws ob that rabbi juice. Dat stuff is tiger blood. You had enough wild time las' night to last you all de res' ob your life does you live fo' evah."

"Wilecat, you sounds right. When us gits to Oaklan' I craves to settle down. Mebbe I shows you a business I aims to 'vest in."

"You don't show me no business, boy. Only business I craves is to find Lily and Lady Luck. Lily's ramblin' loose somewhere in San F'mcisco wid dem Blue Fezant boys. Does I meet up wid dat goat I'll sho' bust him in de haid fo' leavin' me. Every time me an' Lily gits a divo'ce ol' man Hard Luck camps on my trail. Business sounds good, but me, I 'cumulates Lily an' den I takes dem Blue Fezant boys back to Chicago. Mebbe when I comes back heah nex' time us starts some business. Not now. Naw, suh--not me!"

"Wilecat, some business ain't so bad. All you does is set dere an' take in de money."

"All you does is set dere, you mean, an' listen' to some triflin' niggah wantin' groceries or mebbe wantin' to eat whilst you supplies free grub, does you run a restaurant. Dem boys what buys easy never is got money. Naw, suh, I don't want no business, Mud Turtle. All I want is Lady Luck an' mah mascot goat."

The Mud Turtle continued his business dream without paying much attention to the Wildcat's arguments. "Dere's de anti-hair-kink business; all a boy does is buy some things at the drugsto' an' mix 'em up an' sells 'em at fifty cents a bottle. All de niggahs in de worl' craves to buy anti-kink juice. I's seed some remedies what took off de scalp an' some what removes de brain, but it don't make no diff'unce--niggahs keep on buyin', no matteh how deep de remedy digs in."

"Dat business is ol'," the Wildcat objected. "Dat's too ol' to ketch folks any mo'."

"So's kinky hair ol'," answered the Mud Turtle. "Dat business still ketches 'em. While de kinky hair las', so does de anti-kink business. Dat ain't de only business I knows. You an' me had luck wid fish--part bad luck an' part good luck. Here's de ocean an' here's San F'mcisco bay crowded wid fish. 'Spose us gits a wagon an' some hooks fo' ketchin' fish an' comes home eve'y day wid a wagon load."

"Don' say fish to me, boy! All de bad luck I'se had lately come f'm fish. See kin you talk 'bout some good-luck business does yo' crave to. Ah ain't got oveh mah fish luck yit."

"How 'bout de boot-leggin' business, Wilecat? Dey sho' is big money in dat."

"Nobody to sell to no mo'. Eve'ybody's boot-leggin' now. You steps up to a man on de street an' says 'How 'bout it?' an' he thinks you's tryin' to buy. Eve'ybody's boot-leggin'! See kin you think ob some business what's got some customers, instead ob eve'ybody runnin' de business deyself. Naw, suh, I aims not to let no business 'flooence me. I rounds me up Lily an' meets up wid Lady Luck, an' someday I sees ol'

Cap'n Jack agin', an' den I quits worryin'. What I craves mos' is to
ketch Lily an' den git some regulah run where I sleeps mos' all de
time. 'Less I fin's mah mascot I aims to quit de whole Pullman business
an' let 'em git on de bes' dey can widout me."

"Boy, how come you so tame? When we lef' Poteland all you talked about
was startin' a sinful life an' bustin' all de speed records on de road
to hell. Now all you craves is to settle down. Has de itch got you?
'Pears like you needs quinine."

"I don' need nuthin' 'ceptin' Lily an' Lady Luck--an' mebbe a slug o'
gin."

"Cain't git no gin now days."

"Mud Turtle, when us gits to Oaklan' you follow me. I'll bet dat rabbi
boy what chefs on dis train knows whah at is some gin. Any man what kin
throw a dose ob hoof oil together on short notice what makes a nigger
look like a cyclone sho' can dig up a drink o' gin. Quick as us gits to
Oakland I trails 'at boy down. Chances is he starts de rabbi business
soon as he gits his apron off. I depends on him fo' gin. I's jined up
wid de chu'ch when I was sixteen, but now I aims to git backslid back
enough to take de road what leads into dis rabbi place. You goes in an'
takes off yo' hat, an' as quick as you gits baptized, the ol' preacheh
says, 'Boys, what'll it be?' I says, 'Make mine gin.' Ol' Mud Turtle
say, 'Make mine gin.' We says 'at 'bout six times, an' away us goes
lookin' fo' Lily. At's better'n any business talk you'se talkin'."

"I'll say so, Wilecat--fo'get de business. Us has money, anyhow.
There's that fo' hund'ed dollahs you give me an' whatever you'se got
left off de Spindlin' Spider boy you cleaned in Poteland. I agrees wid
you--fo'get de business."

With the arrival of the train in Oakland, about four minutes sufficed to clear up the Mud Turtle's official obligations to the company. Immediately thereafter he and the Wildcat set out to overtake the dining car chef, whom they had seen leaving the terminal. The Wildcat edged up beside the rabbi. "Boy," he said, "how 'bout some licker? Me an' the Mud Turtle here craves to git baptized wid a couple o' slugs o' gin. Is de gin included in de rabbi business?"

The chef looked at the Wildcat. "Us rabbis handles some gin, but it sho' comes high."

"Boy, us aims to pay high. You ain't talkin' to no busted steamboat niggahs. Us ain't fiel' han's. Me an' my podneh got money; all we craves is gin."

The chef's gaze left the Wildcat's face for a moment and seemed to travel to some more distant point. The Wildcat's statement of his finances had aroused the rabbi's cupidity. "Come on heah," he said briefly.

The three made their way up town and presently entered the door of a ramshackle structure standing midway of a block lined by similar buildings. They walked into a darkened room, and the Wildcat saw a fresco of gleaming white eyeballs ranged about him.

"Whah at is us?" he asked the rabbi.

"Dis heah's de Oaklan' Pleasure Club, sort of a social off-shot f'm de chu'ch."

"What chu'ch?"

"Chu'ch is called Banded Brothehs ob de Loose Barrel Hoop. I rabbis fo' dem when I's in town. When I'se away dey's got another boy what does de rabbi work."

The chef turned to the assemblage. "Boys, meet up wid de Mud Turtle. I 'spec' some o' you all knows him. Dis heah other boy travels under de name ob de Wilecat."

A voice from a corner of the room bellered into the midst of the assemblage. "What'll it be, boys? Dis is on de Wilecat."

The Wildcat put on the financial brakes. "How come?"

"Dis heah's de initiation drink. Eve'ybody what joins de Banded Brothehs buys a drink fo' de congregation."

The Wildcat's eyes had become more accustomed to the darkness. "'Pears like I gits lifted fo' goin' on fo'ty drinks."

Presently half a dozen bottles were mingling around with the congregation, and the Wildcat's words to the Mud Turtle beside him were drowned in a chorus of gurgling throats. The gulping ceased. Out of an obscure corner of the room came the Auditor's tones. "Eighty-two dollars. Wilecat, pay me befo' de long green gits wilted."

The Wildcat was no piker, but the bill hit him pretty hard. "I's seen saloons you could buy complete fo' half de money," he remonstrated. He walked over to where a narrow square of light broke through the wall. He fished out a big roll of bills from which he proceeded to count ninety dollars. He replaced the money in his pocket. As he did so a yellow electric light flashed in another part of the room and burned steadily above a small table upon which was stretched a green cloth. A man beside the table called to the newcomer. "Wilecat, de pleasure part ob de entertainment now starts. Now you gits action."

"How come action? Action what wid?"

"Action wid de freckled bones what knows 'rithmetic."

The Wildcat accepted the invitation. Here was a chance to retrieve the price of the drinks. He walked over to the corner. "Whah at's de bones?"

In allowing his opponent to supply the weapons he had committed a serious technical error, but the only other dice in the crowd were the taper cubes belonging to the Mud Turtle, and the Wildcat knew that the production of these dice in that congregation would probably result in his immediate disintegration under the blades of some hungry social razors.

The boy on the opposite side of the table spoke. "Shoots fifty dollahs!"

"You sho' starts blooded." The Wildcat peeled fifty dollars from his roll. "You'se faded. Roll 'em."

The boy rolled them, and an ace-dooce bloomed under the electric light.

A grunt of disappointment went up from several interested veterans of the Banded Brothers gathered around the table, and the rabbi plunged his way into the crowd. He used a few words not commonly included in a rabbi's vocabulary. "Git out o' de way. Gimme dem dice. How come you makes dis mistake?" He took the dice from the loser. "Wilecat, Ah shoots fifty dollars!"

The Wildcat divided his winnings and laid fifty dollars on the table. "Rabbi, roll 'em."

The rabbi breathed a fervent prayer upon the speckled cubes and cast them away from him into the outer darkness. "Freckle tops, git right! Bam! I reads seven. Lets it lay. Shoots a hund'ed!"

"Roll 'em, you'se faded." The Wildcat trimmed himself for another hundred.

The rabbi made another throw. "Luck dice, ketch dat Wilecat. Whuff! An' dey says five an' a six. Dey sho' is lucky."

The Wildcat grunted. "Lucky fo' you."

"Pussonel luck is de luck I likes best," the rabbi returned. "I lets it lay. You has yo' chance. Shoots two hund'ed."

The Wildcat skinned his roll for two hundred dollars. "Dese heah frog skins sho' has got de quick dwindles. You'se faded. Roll 'em."

The rabbi abandoned his ecclesiastical lingo and fell into the vernacular. "Tiger dice, claw me! Turtle dice, off de log! Soap dice, git slick. Clean dat Wilecat. Gun dice, pull de triggah--wham! An' I reads six-ace."

The Wildcat's fingers began to itch for the possession of the bones. He turned to the Mud Turtle, who was close beside him. "Hot dam, boy, dat talk sho' sounds nat'chul! Dat boy growed up someplace else befo' he started de rabbi business."

The rabbi raked in his winnings. He slipped half the roll and laid it on the green cloth. "Shoots two hund'ed. Fade me is you reckless!"

The Wildcat was in too deep to back out. He pared two hundred dollars from his roll and laid it beside the rabbi's stake. "Boy, yo' luck's got to bus' sometime, even is you a rabbi. Roll 'em an' see kin you roll to de po' house."

The rabbi spoke confidentially to the dice for a few moments and then his voice lifted above the murmur of the congregation. "Snow babies, let de soot specs read seven. Rooster dice, crow de pay call! Hen dice, hatch de money eggs. Mule dice, kick dat boy into de rivah! Bam! An' I reads five-dooce."

This triumph of the rabbi was a signal for a revolt on the part of the Wildcat. "I quits. I craves to handle dem bones pussonal. Does you own 'em all de time I quits."

The rabbi handed a pair of dice to the Wildcat. "Roll 'em does you crave to," he said. The concession was made only after he had switched the dice. The Wildcat got hold of twin dice which were loaded to come out dooce, trey, or twelve on the first throw. He warmed the dice to a functioning temperature in the palm of his right hand. In his left he held the remainder of his roll. He laid the money on the centre of the table. "Shoots it all. Two hund'ed dollars. Fade me, boy."

The rabbi counted out two hundred dollars, but before the Wildcat threw the dice the Mud Turtle beside him spoke up. "I shoots fo' hund'ed on the Wildcat's luck. Shoot's fo' hund'ed. Fade me, boy."

The rabbi grunted and dug into his roll for another four hundred.

The Wildcat turned to the Mud Turtle. "Boy, us is bust does I lose!"

"I been bust befo', Wilecat. So is you. Roll 'em see kin you git double or nuthin'."

The Wildcat said a few words to the dice, and an instant later they rattled across the green cloth. "Cyclone babies, blow dat rabbi to hell! Whuff! An' I reads--ace-dooce. Doggone, Lady Luck, whah at is you?"

The Mud Turtle grabbed the Wildcat by the arm. "Come on heah befo' dey gits yo' clothes."

The Wildcat turned away from the table. "Us sho' needs 'at mascot goat. Was hard luck a minny us done ketched a whale. Trouble wid luck, it's always changin'. Don' stay on de good side long enough fo' a boy to git settled down." He bade farewell to the rabbi. "You sho' was right. I'll say gin comes high. Fo' hund'ed dollars a drink!"

The rabbi laughed a hollow laugh. "Come on back sometime an' try de thousan' dollah gin when you feels strongeh."

"Does I find Lily an' Lady Luck I comes back an' shows you some million-dollar gin--mebbe."

"On your way, boy--at's de quinine talkin'!"

CHAPTER XVI

Launched by the rabbi's parting taunt, the Wildcat and the Mud Turtle made their way out of the ginagogue. On the street the Wildcat set the course toward Twelfth Street. His companion pounded along as best he could for a while and then voiced a protest. "What for is you got such a hot foot?"

"Come on heah, ol' Mud Turtle. I craves to meet up wid dat Lily goat befo' any mo' calamity ketches up wid me."

"Whah you spec' to fin' dat doggone goat?"

"San F'mcisco some place. Ah tol' you once. De Blue Fezant boys went to San F'mcisco on de train, an' de las' I seed ob Lily she was penned up along wid 'bout nine ob dem boys. 'At goat's in San F'mcisco."

"How long you spec' it take you to fin' 'at mascot in San F'mcisco? You know how big 'at town is?"

"Boy, I been dere. I been clear from downtown out to de Presidio whah at dey keeps de ahmy boys an' de gin'rals. I seed 'at town befo'."

The Mud Turtle grunted. "You ain't seed nuthin'. 'At town's ten times 'at big. Was Lily fo' years ol' when you started lookin' she'd be eight hund'ed fo' you foun' her, 'less you had luck."

"Does I fin' her I gits all de luck I needs. Us wins bofe ways, 'cause all de bad luck I could git wouldn't be no worse'n what us has now. I'se plum busted. How is you?"

The Mud Turtle audited the depths of his pocket. "Nuthin' but some ravelin' lint an' fo' bits."

"'At's enough. Don' look so mean, ol' Mud Turtle. Does us see another rabbi walkin' down de main street us better take de alley fo' he sees us. Dem rabbi boys is just like a ticket to de po' house. Dem ginagogue gin rabbis is de wust of all."

At eleven o'clock the pair landed at the ferry building in San

Francisco. As a precaution against lunch money, they saved the change from Mud Turtle's half dollar and walked towards the centre of the town.

They landed finally in Union Square.

The Wildcat flopped down on the grass, and the Mud Turtle joined him. "Mud Turtle, what's dat big house oveh there?" He pointed at the St. Francis Hotel.

"Boy, thought you told me you was here once befo'. Dat's de St. Frantic Hotel."

"How come de boy frantic what dey named de hotel fo'?"

"'Spec' he drunk some hoof oil, o' mebbe met a gin rabbi. Sho' is a fine day."

"All de days I seen in de town was fine days, 'ceptin' some evenin's when de fog gits heavy."

"Ol' fog comes in mighty handy does you owe money. Boy kin lose hisself f'm a bloodhoun' easy in de fog."

The Wildcat stretched himself out and prepared to go to sleep, but before he had accomplished his purpose he was interrupted by his companion.

"Wilecat, look at dem two boys on de hotel steps. Dey sho' looks like dem Blue Fezant Nobles you was speakin' 'bout."

The Wildcat rose to his knees and looked across Powell Street. Sure enough, there before his eyes stood two of the Blue Fezant gentlemen.

He lost no time in going towards them. "Come on heah, Mud Turtle! I knowed we'd meet some o' dem Blue Fezant boys. Come on heah!"

A moment later the Wildcat and the Mud Turtle confronted the two Nobles of the Mysterious Mecca. Each of the nobles was festooned with a golf bag. The pair were headed for Lincoln Park. The Wildcat spoke to the larger of the two gentlemen. "Cap'n, suh," he said, "I was de po'tah on a special car f'm Chicago what hauled some of you Blue Fezant gen'men out heah. Kin you tell me whah at Lily mah mascot goat is?"

The Blue Fezant gentleman looked at the Wildcat for a moment. "Seems to me I heard about that goat. Some of the boys got him some place."

The second man interposed some additional information. "You mean the white goat? He's out with Jim and Frank on the golf links."

The first Potent Noble turned toward the Wildcat. "He's out where we're going now. Come with us and maybe you'll find him. Is he your goat?'

"Cap'n, suh, you sho' soun' good! Does I meet up wid dat Lily I beats 'at goat to death--mebbe. Lily sho' is mah goat. I raised him clean f'm France." He turned to his companion. "Mud Turtle, take 'at bag fo' de gen'men. Cap'n, suh, we carry dis stuff."

The Potent Nobles smiled at each other. "These boys can caddy for us. Do you boys want to caddy for us?"

Without knowing exactly what it was, the Wildcat signed quite a contract. "Cap'n, yessuh. Whatever you wants, us does. How come dis caddy business?"

"You carry the bag around while we go golf hunting."

The Wildcat spoke lowly to the Mud Turtle. "Golf hunting? What's dis heah golfs? Neveh seed one pussonally."

"Boy, don't you know what golfs is? Sumpin' like a dog, only smaller. Born wild. Dey gin'ally gits wilder when dey grows up."

"How big does dey git?"

"Dog size--some bigger, sometimes."

"Neveh seed none in Memphis."

"Dey's tame down dere; out heah dey grows wild. Some parts, de wild golfs run 'roun' so thick a man hardly kin plough his fiel', 'thout carryin' six or eight shotguns on de plow. Dis country was 'fested wid golfs till de Indians got heah."

"'Fested wid Indians till white folks got heah, too. I guess could de Indians kill a golf us is safe."

He turned to one of the Potent Nobles. "Cap'n, suh, what does you kill dese here golfs wid?"

The Noble was quick to take up the deception. "We beat 'em to death with those clubs. If you get a small blue golf, you beat him with an iron club. For the savage red ones you use that club with the piece of brass on it. The whisky golf is the worst, though; he sort of sneaks up on you. You use those little clubs for them. They're called putters. They're shorter so you can use 'em in close places. Short and deadly."

The quartette were presently seated in an automobile which was retrieved from Powell Street. On the way to the Lincoln Park golf course the party detoured through Golden Gate Park. The car drove past the enclosure wherein leaped a dozen full grown kangaroos. One of the Potent Nobles pointed to the awkward animals. "There's some golfs now if you boys never seen any."

A restless kangaroo made a thirty-foot leap. "Lawd Gawd, Cap'n, does you kill dem debbils wid clubs? I craves a cannon an' forty miles' range, or else one o' them airplane flyin' things."

"All you have to do is to stand right close behind me and you'll be safe."

The Wildcat's training had taught him to trust the word of a white man. "Cap'n, yes, suh." As far as he was concerned, the conversation was ended, but in spite of the Potent Noble's reassuring words, a feeling of uneasiness seemed to undermine him.

At the hunting preserves in Lincoln Park it became evident that luck was not with the two golf-killing Nobles of the Mysterious Mecca, because about all these two gentlemen did was to continue the monotonous business of knocking a couple of innocent looking white balls across the landscape. Every now and then they would come upon a grass lawn with an iron cup in the centre of it, and then each Potent Noble would waste a lot of time urging his ball into the cup with the short and deadly putter which was normally used for slaughtering whisky golfs which sneaked up on you.

After the first mile or two the zest of the chase was dulled by the Wildcat's habitual languor. He edged over towards the Mud Turtle. "Mud Turtle, 'spec' dese gen'men gwine to give us fo' bits, mebbe, fo' he'pin 'em hunt dese golfs what we ain't seed. Ah feels dismal. Every time dey shoots 'at ball, s'posin' you an' me shoots ten cents?"

"How come, Wilecat? You knows us cain't monkey wid dis huntin' game."

"I don't mean monkey wid de huntin'," the Wildcat returned. "Is you got a lead pencil? 'Sposin' us marks de li'l white balls wid de dice freckles an' reads 'em when dey drops. Fust you take one time, den I takes anotheh. Us plays some mountain dominoes. Got to do sumpin', else us goes to sleep. Den like as not some ragin' golf sneak up an' eat yo' innards fo' you has a chance to wake up. Le's try shootin' some sevens at de scenery."

Action followed the Wildcat's words, and presently the two golf balls then in use were marked with a pattern of black dots running from the gentle ace to the belligerent six spot. Thereafter the two Potent Nobles had reason to wonder at the sudden industry exhibited by their caddies, who leaped after each ball almost before the club had touched it.

"Bam! Look at that boy go, Jim! I wish we could get caddies like that in Chicago; the lazy devils never would go after a ball. These fellows are bears."

"They're all good,--the best caddies I ever had were niggers in the south,--after you get 'em woke up, that is."

Meanwhile, out at the destination of the golf ball the Wildcat and the Mud Turtle were inspecting it where it lay. "Three up." The pair raced to the point where the other ball had fallen. "She reads fo'. Fo' an' three is seven. Wilecat, doggone you, you wins again."

"Sho' I wins! Didn' dem Blue Fezant boys say dis heah mascot goat ob mine was roustin' roun' out heah? Whaheveh dat goat is, so is Lady Luck. Fo' long I meets up wid Lily, an' den I shows you some winnin' what is."

The two Potent Nobles holed out at the ninth, and the party crossed the road under the trees to the tenth tee. "Cap'n, suh," the Wildcat asked, "what's 'at rock oveh dah, widout no roof an' de rock wall?"

The Potent Noble looked over at the Chinese tomb. "That's where some Chinaman is buried," he said. "That's a Chinese tomb."

"Tomb! Some dead boy layin' in it?"

"I'll say so--maybe a dozen of 'em. This whole golf pasture is built over a graveyard."

The Wildcat stiffened and looked at the Mud Turtle. "Lawd Gawd, Mud Turtle! Us cravin' to meet Lady Luck an' walkin' 'roun' in a graveyard! Sho' makes me dwindle up inside! No wondeh dem man-eatin' golfs is so ragin' out heah. Wish I could fin' dat doggone Lily Goat." He turned to one of the Potent Nobles. "Ain't we startin' down town, Cap'n, fo' it gits dark?"

"It'll be two hours yet before it gets dark. We've got time to hunt another golf or two. Shut up while I drive."

"Cap'n, yessuh."

At the sixteenth tee the Potent Noble looked down at the heavy fog which was rolling in through the Golden Gate. He addressed the ball. He jumbled around on his feet and took a couple of practice swings. Perfection was in every movement. Then, as he drove, the Wildcat sneezed. There followed a blast of profanity whose equal the Wildcat had not heard since his army days. He edged over towards the Mud Turtle. "Neveh seed a boy change so quick. Heah he is, pleasant one minnit, an' den he hits dat ball an' goes hog wild. Seems like--"

He was interrupted by the Potent Noble, who had calmed down. "Git the hell out in the rough there and find that ball I sliced."

"Yes, suh." The Wildcat started out through the fog to find the freckled white sphere. He threshed around in the trees and underbrush for a while, and then to his mind came a memory of the horrible words which the Potent Noble had spoken. "This place was a graveyard!" The Wildcat shuddered extensively and abandoned the search for the golf ball.

He looked up, and there before him was a tombstone!

"Lawd Gawd, Lady Luck, whah is you?" Automatically his feet began to work, and they were aided an instant later by his racing legs. He went away from there through the fog. The next thing he knew, he had made a forty-foot dive over a sand bank. He rolled for a moment in the shifting sand before he brought up against a stunted cedar.

"Whah at is I?"

The fog cleared, and the Wildcat saw the sand dunes stretching below him. At the edge of the slope were the waves of the Golden Gate. Then the fog closed in again, and everything about him faded out of the picture. Above his head, out of the drifting fog, a flight of sea gulls started a little gossip. To the Wildcat's ears came their shrieking remarks. He stopped his wild shuddering and began to moan.

"'At's dem ghost boys! I know 'em! Lady Luck, take dem boys away. I ain't talkin' wid no ghosts." He turned and started up the bank. He began throwing sand out from under his feet like a record-busting rotary snow plough. His legs ran for ten minutes, but his wind was crippled, and in the shifting sand he covered a space of less than twenty feet. Exhausted with his effort, he flopped down on the sloping bank. "Dey's got me," he moaned, "dey's got me! I knowed it. I knowed dem graveyard ghosts would git me, once I gits divo'ced fum dat mascot goat. Lady Luck, here I is!" The Wildcat curled up and covered his head with his arms.

He lay in repose for less than ten seconds; for suddenly, out of the fog in mid channel, came the booming siren whistle of a liner, heading out of the Golden Gate. "Whoom! Wha-om!"

The Wildcat moaned. "I heahs you, Gabriel, I heahs you! Heah I is, Lawd--heah I is."

"Whooom! We-ow-oom!"

"It's me. It's ol' Wilecat. What fo' you askin' who? You knows who! Ghosts got me, Gabriel! Here I is! Lady Luck--Good-bye!"

Then from Fort Miley crashed the report of the evening gun that marked retreat, and a moment later the clear notes of a bugle floated out of the fog. For a moment life on earth again claimed the Wildcat, and instinctively he responded to his army training. He got to his feet and stood rigidly at attention. Into the fog to an unseen company he yelled a series of commands. "Come to 'tenshun! Silence in de ranks! Shut up an' stan' up! 'Tenshun! Lily, come to 'tenshun! Cap'n Jack, suh, de company is fo'med."

He saluted and made an about-face as perfectly as he could in the shifting sand beneath his feet.

As he did so he felt his brain rattle. Ten feet above him, tangible as iron, real as gold, festooned with hair and horns, stood Lily the mascot goat.

The Wildcat stood fixed for an instant looking with incredulous eyes at the mascot. Then he made an excess demand on the motor muscles of his legs, and in six wild leaps he had gained the goat's side.

"Lily, is you back? Goat, hot dam! Lady Luck sho' heard me!" The Wildcat grabbed the leading string which dangled from the mascot's neck. "Come heah--I aims to git me some han'-cuffs an' lock one end 'roun yo' neck an' de otheh roun' mah laig. Goat, us sho' is proud to meet up wid you! Does you leave me once mo' nex' time I knocks yo' hawns down yo' throat."

Lily evidently approved the arrangement. She looked at the Wildcat, and then from her skinny throat a faint bleat sounded.

"Say dat again! You sounds noble!"

"Blaaa," answered Lily.

The Wildcat looked around him. His fear of the shrieking ghostly voices from the sky overhead had melted into the fog. No longer did the howling devils of mid channel disturb him. No longer did he fear the raging golf. With his mascot goat at his side, no evil luck could touch him. Courage returned, and with it extravagant language. "Lily, no doggone ghos' better git uppity wid me. I'd bus' a ol' ghos' in de haid did I ketch one."

With Lily beside him, he gained the level ground of the fairway. Then, over a wide expanse of golf links, the fog had lifted clear. The Wildcat saw the two Blue Fezant Nobles poking around near the Chinese tomb in search of the ball which had been lost a little while before.

"Come on heah, Lily." He dragged the mascot to the Chinese tomb, near which the Mud Turtle was halted.

"Ain't you foun' 'at little white ball yit, Mud Turtle?"

"Not me, Wilecat. Dat ball landed inside dis heah graveyard tomb. You don't git me in dere fo' a million dollahs. What's 'at! You foun' yo' goat!"

"Boy, out o' mah way!" The Wildcat walked toward the Chinese tomb as fast as Lily could cover the ground. "Git out o' mah way. Me an' Lily looks in dat tomb place. Us ain't scared o' no ol' ghosts no mo'."

One of the Blue Fezant gentleman called to the Wildcat. "Son, where in hell have you been?"

Something in the Potent Noble's tone made the Wildcat think of Captain Jack and the gone-away days in France. "Cap'n, suh, no place. I was jes' 'cumulatin' mah mascot goat."

He entered the roofless Chinese tomb, and there on the stone floor lay the golf ball. "Cap'n, suh," he yelled, "heah's yo' freckled pill." He called less loudly to the Mud Turtle. "Oteh ball read three. Dis one heah's got de fo' spot up. 'At's seven! Mud Turtle, you loses. Come in heah an' look at it."

The Mud Turtle's dread of the Chinese tomb was still with him. "I 'cepts yo' word fo' it, Wilecat. Doggone you. Boy, you wins fo' times runnin'."

"Boy, f'm now on I wins steady. Lady Luck done sent back mah mascot goat. I cain't lose!"

He turned to his four-legged companion. "Kin us, Lily, whilst you's wid me?"

"Blaaa!" answered Lily. "I should say not."

CHAPTER XVII

1.

> "Lead me to de woods whah de luck trees grow,
> Han' me de axe when it's time to chop.
> Lead me kinda gentle,--git me started slow;
> When I gits to goin', watch de luck trees drop."

While the Wildcat was doing his best to forget the cares that nominally infested his official day as porter on the Blue Fezant special car, sidetracked in San Francisco, Honey Tone Boone, the brunet uplifteh, languished in the Memphis jail.

There were two sides to every jail. To the Wildcat, the loser in the law's game generally occupied the inside. Honey Tone was different. The inside of a jail for Honey Tone was often a place of sanctuary from which the occupant might sneer serenely at the disappointed female perils who gnashed their teeth outside the bars.

In San Francisco the days were warm, and Lily the mascot goat had returned to her master's side.

The Wildcat was playing even in the matter of daily rations. Trailing along in the wake of a pair of the golf-playing Nobles of the Mysterious Mecca at the Lincoln Park Golf course provided a cash

surplus which enabled the Wildcat to discard his winter-weight Prince
Albert and to adorn his person with a retiring suit of clothes three
shades lighter than a sunburned pumpkin and embellished with six-inch
checks. Life wasn't so bad. Ol' railroad sleepin' car was probably
doin' all right. Reasonably sure that tomorrow would lug in new brands
of trouble to pester a boy with, the Wildcat steered his somnolent
mentality clear of the shoals of surmise and let tomorrow take care of
itself.

A boy never could tell about Lady Luck. Every time the Wildcat did
something that clearly entitled him to free board in some permanent
jail, like as not next day he would wake up all festooned with gold
watches. Take a preacher's advice and head down the straight and narrow
path, and the chances were that some deppity sherriff with a shotgun,
or else a bear, would be waiting in the path right where the heaviest
canebrakes discouraged detours.

2.

    "One man's pizen is anotheh man's meat,--
    Mah troubles neveh botheh you.
    Hog needs wings like a snake needs feet:
    De question ain't why, but who."

Honey Tone Boone's downfall had been accomplished in Memphis
immediately subsequent to a Konk'rin' Heroes' parade. There had been
some talk about the ownership of the mule which Honey Tone rode. The
line of march headed straight for Honey Tone's wife and his potential
soul mate and culminated in a ruckus from which Honey Tone emerged,
safe in the talons of a policeman. The two women, comparing notes, had
gummed up the leader's grand entry to a degree which left Honey Tone
thankful for the mule-stealing charge that had landed him safe in the

jail and out of the clutches of his wife and Cuspidora Lee. He enjoyed sanctuary in jail for two months and then, threatened with an embarrassing and abrupt release, he concentrated on a hurried mental incubation. Hard pressed, he sought to hatch from the bad egg of circumstance some new enterprise which would take him away, sudden and safe, from where his memorizing wife awaited him.

His mind roamed wild through the fields of questionable enterprises opened to him by a combination of easy conscience and the flashy part of a "college" education. On the day of his release he half regretted his education. Ignorance cursed the individual with work, but it left him free of the higher responsibilities and the more acute penalties of transgressions, and just then Honey Tone wished devoutly that he was a field hand. He craved a black complexion instead of the halfway colour that barred him from the unquestioning comradeship of white and black alike.

On the night of his release from jail he beat the barrier, and by morning he was well on his way to St. Louis, resolved to explore the Pacific coast for fields wherein his peculiar abilities might enable him to reap the harvest of cash without which life to him was naught.

En route West, Honey Tone managed to keep one state ahead of his reputation. Thus he avoided the iron impedimenta which the laws of the land drape around the ankles and feet that stray from the straight and narrow trail--around wrists and hands whose idleness affords the devil welcome opportunity to function as a labour agent.

Honey Tone's first week in Oakland found him preaching to a small congregation. On the following Sunday he announced to his flock that subscriptions for a church building fund would be accepted, beginning forthwith.

"Temp'rary an' perm'nent." The announcement followed a long prayer during which the uplifter's face wore the same holy expression as that which adorns the first stages of a sneeze. "Rev'und" Honey Tone Boone opened his eyes and tamed his vocabulary to the vernacular current among his hearers. "Temp'rary an' perm'nent. Weekly refun's on all temp'rary subscriptions, togetheh with int'res' at a hund'ed per cent. You doubles yo' 'vestment, like de boy wid de ten talents."

The dangling bait was presently engulfed.

The subscription books were kept open throughout the week. Facilities for subscribing were offered through agencies established in the pastor's quarters, in two barber shops and three pool rooms.

On the following Sunday, after a service devoted largely to discussion of temporal problems which afflict the flesh here in this vale of tears, Honey Tone paid his subscribers their original contributions and added an equal sum for interest at a hund'ed per cent.

The books were flooded with new subscriptions within the next fifteen minutes. The six agencies did a rushing business all during the week. On Friday Honey Tone counted his cash and decided that another week could be managed. Then--exit.

After the next Sunday services, owing to an eight that looked like a three, he was short five hundred dollars in the item of interest.

Explanations led to retreat, and Honey Tone retreated to a hotel in San Francisco. His flight therefrom was interrupted by a delegation from a mob which visited him on the following night. He beat the delegation out of the lobby of the hotel because, in the emergency, his feet acted more quickly than his head. He went away from there leading his flock.

Mentally he shipped his remains to his next of kin four times in the next fifty yards. Out of the corner of his eye he caught the gleam of a piece of light-coloured steel swung by a dark-coloured investor who craved to collect his investment, plus interest, one way or another.

Honey Tone's racing legs, impelled by an acute ambition, functioned successfully in their owner's single endeavour to lead the flying wedge of razor-bearing blood hunters by at least two jumps more than a slashin' reach. The fugitive turned into Mission Street; and here in the long stretch the saddle-coloured financier saw a chance to do some thinking. Galloping was his main business just then, but he carried a side line of quick thoughts.

With members of his own race Honey Tone asked no greater odds in the money game than those which served from the theory that mind was superior to matter. But in this, too, time was the essence. Just then he needed time. Ten minutes were worth a million dollars and lots of other important things like health and strength and blood. Time was that without which the best laid plans died in the egg.

For the next five blocks, running something less than a mile a minute, the uplifter's brain functioned with the cunning which enables the fragrant fox to overcome the handicap with which nature has equipped him, when the hounds begin the cross country obesity cure. During this time a plan had flowered in Honey Tone's brain whereby victory might be snatched from what had looked like a total loss of all the blood that would run out of where a razor had nestled.

In a shadowed area midway between two street lights Honey Tone stopped. He stopped abruptly, like a golf ball hitting the north side of Gibraltar. He bounced back, absorbing his momentum in a twisting motion which left him squarely facing the oncoming pack. Now it was, or never!

When they were upon him he raised his arms.

He orated. "Hush! Git calm! Now us kin talk! Money! Cash! Rest easy!"

His voice lifted one notch higher than the undertone which welled about him. The peak load of peril was confronted and passed, but still his speech ranged over the bait words most potent as verbal sedatives. "Easy money--lissen--gin--seven dice--fancy clothes--chicken an' gin fo' one an' all soopreem members."

He discarded his college-bred dialect and adopted the vernacular of the majority about him. "Lissen heavy! Git calm. Len' me yo' ears. Men an' brethren, you knows me. Fo'gettin' de peril o' de tar bar'l an' de p'cessions at night wid blazin' pitch knots an' de chokin' rope whut folks uses when dey uprises, an' chosin' fo' ouah guide de lives ob de ol'-time martyrs, safe an' serene in de circle ob fate cast 'roun' mah fragile form by dis yere rabbit's foot--Ah tells you--lissen!"

The speaker waved his rabbit's foot. He beckoned at the loose fringe of sceptics which milled on the margin of the group. "Gether together, dat ye can hear de words ob wisdom. De prophet knowed whut he said when he perdicted dat somebody was comin' to lead his chillun f'm darkness into light. 'At's me! Somebody. I leads you out ob darkness into de promised lan' whah flows de milk an' honey. In passin' lemme add dat milk is f'm de ol' language used by de Sanskrits, meanin' gin. Honey f'm de ancient Check-Slowfat word 'Honito.' Dat's de word fo' chicken--fried chicken, to be mo' preciser.... Men, you is sons ob Kings f'm Africa. How come you all redoosted to de state ob slaves? How come bird shot cain't pester a cinnamon bear? Because yo' brains and yo' brawns is all spread out, desiccated on triflin' things like cotton crops an' cawn, sweatin' undeh heavy loads 'stid of rulin' at de seat of guv'ment an' dictatin' whut's whut."

The orator dragged in another lungful of midnight fog and broke into the stretch. "Heah's de answeh, graved on de gol' tablets an' dug up in de midnight moon wid a luck spade. Gran' oaks f'm li'l acorns grow. Heah in San F'mcisco wid de aid of you all we starts de new movement towards de Canaan land. Fust off, us o'ganizes de Temple o' Luck. Den de fust annex is de Swamick Chu'ch, based on de mystic teachin' of Swami de Indian Budda. Nex' do' in de Temple de Soopreem Faith Healer thrives an' collects money f'm folks whut only thinks dey's sick. 'Cross de hall is de Chief Palm Readin' Magi, predictin' pas', present, an' future fo' a dollah. In de Temple Annex is de offices ob de 'Filiated Culled Union ob de worl'. Dis Union is mitigated into th'ee gran' divisions--de Bullshevik, de P'litical, an' de Social. De Social has de Ladies' Annex."

Honey Tone's eyes played steadily across his audience, horizontally, and his voice shot straight at the ears of the assemblage, but his imagination started up, and now it made its final flight. "Dat's all I tells you, 'ceptin' my own humble efforts will be directed at organizin' a New World Af'ican Colony in de free country of Barzil. Dat's all. Fo' each an' ev'ry project us needs a Deppity Soopreem Leadeh. Dese will be 'pointed f'm amongst you. Each Deppity Soopreem Leadeh adorns hisself wid de gilt-edge robes ob de 'propriate responsibility an' collects de cash. Deppity Collector fo' each Deppity Leadeh likewise weahs de robes whut de ritual describes. Ritual c'mmittee gits a percentage ob de receipts. Deppities gits one dollah fo' ev'ry three whut's took in. Any income oveh twenty dollahs a day goes to de Social an' Festive departments."

The orator pulled a little book out of his pocket. "Hopin' you elects steady an' reliable frien's fo' de 'sponsible offices, us now opens de 'scription books fo' de Temple Fund, payin' int'rest a hund'ed per cent ev'y week. Pussonally, I donates a hund'ed dollars to staht de ball rollin'--"

Honey Tone knew his crowd.

"How much, brotheh? Sign yo' name. Cash. C'tificate in green an' yaller wid de gol' seal will be conferred at de Fust Conclave ob de Soopreem Leadehs of Departments an' de Gran' Deppities.... Gimme dat bill; I has change, brotheh...."

Late that night, escorted by a committee a little more soopreem than the body of the mob, Honey Tone walked back to his hotel room. Everything was organized to a degree which had deprived the mob of blood hunters of all of their ready cash.

On his way to the hotel the uplifter pondered the question of conduct affecting his immediate future. "To blow or not to blow"--that was the question. He reviewed the hills and valleys of the land of promise over which his galloping vocal organs had hauled the hopes of his hearers. He decided that the business of making good would involve considerable work. The work part failed to attract him. He decided to bid the committee a long farewell at the hotel, without their knowing it, but his decision suffered a veto in the persistence with which the three Soopreem Deppities stuck to their walking treasury department.

In his room Honey Tone made a final effort to side-step the escort. He removed his coat and hung it on a chair. "Now wid de cares whut infests de day relegated to de bosom ob de past, I lays me down an' sleeps. Brothehs, I hopes you all enjoys de boon ob ol' lady nature's sweet restorer, an' I sees you tomorr' at--"

"You sees us now." A heavy-set deppity grunted a verdict. "Gimme 'at quilt, an' I makes down mah pallet on de flo'."

Without implying anything pussonal, another of the soopreem trio laid himself down close against the door.

The uplifter knew a bear trap when he saw it. He pillowed his rangy jaw on the comforting outlines of the lumpy treasure in the pocket of his vest, folded beneath his head. "Talk sure is cheap," he reflected. "Talk is cheap, but sometimes you can trade big words for big money."

A violent snore answered him, and again hope mounted to his heart, but presently he realized that only one of his associates was sleeping.

With the sleepers changing shifts every hour or so, the long night passed.

By dawn Honey Tone was resolved to give his schemes a run for their money. You never could tell how a scheme might turn out; and the colonization business sounded pretty good, even to its overstressed inventor.

CHAPTER XVIII

1.

The convention of the Nobles of the Mysterious Mecca dwindled into the final stage that attends all conventions. Golf was eliminated, and business was the order of the day. The Mud Turtle left him; and thereafter the Wildcat suffered indirectly, being threatened with a resumption of his responsibility as porter on the special car that had brought the Chicago contingent west to San Francisco. A sense of restraint gradually killed off the wild free business of roaming the

Lincoln Park golf course at so much per roam, eating heavy on the proceeds, and sleeping twelve hours a day.

Arrayed in his yaller raiment, he sought the offices of the Pullman company and got confidential with the office boy. "I's de po'teh fo' de blue fezant boys--dis heah Mysterious Mecca business. Dey tells me us leaves fo' Chicago real soon. Ah jus' been down at de deepo lookin' fo' de cah. Whah at is dat cah? Me 'an Lily aims to git it swep' out befo' de gen'men comes."

The office boy took the Wildcat's message to an inner office. Two minutes later the answer came back in the person of a gentleman who was trying to hold his temper. "You're fired! You started with your car in Chicago, left it in Wyoming, and here you are! Git out of here before I--"

"Cap'n, yessuh!" The Wildcat knew a gesture when he saw it. He retreated, dragging his mascot goat a little too fast for Lily's comfort.

"Goat, doggone you, whut fo' did you go A.W.O.L. an' git us bofe loose f'm dat railroad job? Heah us is wid only fo' bits, an' all yo' fault."

Lily admitted the charge in a plaintive bleat which softened the harsh language which her master was bellowing at his mascot in the din of Market Street. Presently the Wildcat forgot the acute misery of not having any hard work staring him in the face. "Us has fo' bits. 'Ats mo' money dan mos' folks has. Lily, us eats.

"I don't bother work, work don't bother me.
I'se fo' times as happy as a bumble bee.
Us eats when us kin git it, sleeps mos' all de time--"

At a lunch counter on Sutter Street much frequented by members of his race the Wildcat spread the fifty cents out over rations that made up in mass what they lacked in delicacy. Half way through the meal he slacked up enough to get talkative. The boy next to him at the lunch counter was confronted with enough food to hold him for a few minutes; and it was at this more fortunate individual that the Wildcat directed his remarks. "Podneh, whah at kin a boy locate a job of work in dis yere town?"

"Whah you f'm?"

"Me an' mah mascot hails f'm Memphis."

"How come you so fah f'm home?"

"Boy, whah at did you meet up wid so much wantin' to know?"

"Good many jail niggers loose. Thought maybe--"

"Don't think no mo'. Don't think 'nuther word 'bout me an' Lily. I come f'm de ahmy. Two yeahs in France, an' lately I lef' de Pullman railroad people whut hires sleepin' cah po'tehs. 'At's all. Ain't no jail connected wid me. All I craves is a job whut pays money."

"De wages at de docks unloadin' steamboats is ten dollahs a day. Depen's on how much money you needs. Dey wants stevedores bad. Dey's a strike."

"Boy, dey has me! I'se a bad stevedo'. Whah at is dis boat-unloadin' bizness?"

The boy revealed the location of the ten-dollar job. "You trails along afteh you gits to de wateh whah de big boats is. Half a mile f'm de ferry buildin' you sees a gang standin' round. Them's strikers. You goes through, an' de boss shows you whah to head in. Does you know de stevedo' business?"

"I'll say us does. Me an' de res' ob de Fust Service Battalion unloaded all de boats whut landed in France durin' de wah. How come you ain't workin' yo'self at de ten-dollah job?"

"I'se a 'vestor. 'Vested some cash in a new o'ganization whut was instigated heah lately. Pays big. Two fo' one ev'y week. You gives de ol' Soopreem Leadeh fifty dollahs, an' nex' week back he comes wid a hund'ed. You hol's out some an' 'vests de res'. Nex' week you reaps agin. Pays fifty, gits a hund'ed."

"Whah at is dis Soopreem man?"

"Thought you tol' me you was broke. How come you lie so?"

"Ain't said no lie."

"You's broke, ain't you? What good does dis Soopreem man do you 'less you kin 'vest wid him? Git yo' job, an' when you has beginnin' money I meets you an' reveals whah at is de gol' mine."

"Meet you heah nex' Sat'dy night. 'At's pay night, I s'poses."

"You s'poses right. Ah meets you Sat'day."

"Sho' will. Podneh, whut name is you favored with? I goes by name Wilecat--by rights I was baptized Vitus Marsden." The Wildcat held out the hand of brotherhood.

"Call me Trombone when you calls confidential," his companion replied. "By rights I is Pike Canfield, but folks calls me Trombone eveh since me an' de name got famous. Mebbe you is heard of me. I plays de slip horn."

"Sho' I is--many's de time! So you is Trombone, is you? Sho' proud to meet up wid you. Sho' 'bliged fo' de knowledge concernin' de ten-dollah job. Soon as I 'cumulates some payday me an' Lily meets you heah nex' Sat'day night. Den us 'vests wid de Soopreem Leadeh an' mebbe has a gran' ruckus wid de profits."

That night the Wildcat slept free and chilly on a park bench, covered only with the blanket of fog which rolled in at midnight.

Shortly after dawn, with Lily at his heels, he walked to the entrance of the pier against which lay a cargo ship loading for a famine area in Europe. "Whah at is de man whut hires de han's?" he asked.

Two hours later the foreman of the dock gang was pointed out to him, and in ten minutes, with Lily tied to a barrel of nutritious pickles, the Wildcat took his place in the long line of stevedores that hustled freight out of the pier shed and into the nets under the cargo booms of the ship. "Lily--tonight us eats on credit, an' sleeps inside some place whah de fog weatheh don't git."

All the stevedore crew were members of the Wildcat's own race. Before noon he had affiliated with enough friends to make the matter of noontime lunch a simple business of accepting part of what was offered him, while Lily did the best she could on enough assorted nutriment to feed six mascots.

Considering the start he had made that morning, the Wildcat realized, with his seventh sandwich, that life isn't so bad if you manage to live

through it. When he began the afternoon shift his ancient philosophy
had returned, and to the clatter of the activity about him he
contributed his rambling voice. Presently the words of his song
recruited a few converts from the gang about him; and by four o'clock,
with the freight moving faster than it had for many a day, the hollow
spaces in the long pier were filled with the echoes that lifted from an
intermittent chorus which proclaimed that

> "I kin load a steamboat, load it full wid freight;
> I kin load a steamboat when it's leavin' late.
> Dat's de reason I'se as happy as a bee,
> I don't botheh work, an' work don't botheh me."

Throughout the late hours of the afternoon the eyes of the foreman were
on the Wildcat. "Hustlin' nigger. Make him a straw boss tomorrow if
this keeps up."

2.

Honey Tone realized that rank imposes commensurate obligation before
his Temple of Luck campaign had lived a week. Too much rank imposed too
much obligation, and so the Swamic Church and the Faith Healing and the
Palm Reading Magi and several other verbal branches of his project were
discarded before the several deppity soopreem leaders got too soopreem
to handle. The backbone of his income was at once the Temple Fund; and
this important business demanded and received all of his energy except
that demanded by his elaborate pictures of the New World African Colony
in Brazil.

The Temple Fund, paying all investors a hundred per cent a week, was
popular from the start. On the first dividend day Honey Tone made the
grade without difficulty, and all subscriptions were repaid, together

with a bonus of a like amount. Immediately after the ceremony of repayment was completed, the backwash of investment began to roll in, and by the evening the promoter counted more than a thousand dollars in his hip pocket treasury. On the next day a new group of subscribers to whom the news had been retailed milled about the doors of the temporary Temple for a chance to register and donate their investments. Honey Tone, operating in a rented house, herded the investors into a room where his voice could pulverize the sediment of reluctance which remained in his hearers' minds, leaving no dregs of doubt that might cloud the nectar of hope.

He donned a serious looking coat, long and black, and swept a broad yellow sash across his chest. On his head rested a Manchu mandarin cap purchased in Chinatown and revised with ornament suitable for the insignia of the Soopreemest. About his waist was the equator part of a Sam Brown belt, and from it dangled a Civil War cavalry sabre whose scabbard had suffered two coats of gilt paint, not quite dry. He retained his ordinary street shoes; life was a battle, and you never could tell when the bugles of fate might blow recall. Street shoes came in handy when there was any heavy running to be done.

In his uniform he addressed the herded investors. "Breth'rin, de books is closed fo' de present week. All whut paid yistiddy gits dey money back, 'long wid de same amout fo' intres' nex', Satidy mawnin'. Dem whut pays de 'scriptions now gits de 'vestment an' de hund'ed per cent intres' de Satidy afteh nex'. De books is now open, de gol' seal c'tificates is ready. Fawm in line an' git yo' money ready.... Ten dollahs, brotheh. Heah's yo' papeh. Now you is a Deppity Soopreem Leadeh, 'titled to de red sash.... Nex' Satidy us 'lects de ten Soopreem Gov'nors fo' de leadin' districts in de New Worl' African Colony at Barzil. Boat leaves wid de 'ficials an' de p'visions nex' month. 'Lection is by de lucky numbehs. Soopreem 'ficials gits a house an' ten thousan' milrice--dat's Barzil dollahs--ev'y month to travel

roun' wid an' see is de distric' doin' O.K.... Fifteen dollahs--dat
'titles you to de Yaller Sash of Trust. Chances is you sho' will be a
Soopreem Gov'nor. Nex' brotheh...."

On the following Saturday Honey Tone managed to postpone the election
of the Soopreem Governors for the ten districts of the colony and to
sidestep the various vague promises that he had sown so lavishly
throughout the preceding two weeks, but in the department of finance
there was no evasion, short of flight, and in the white light that
forever beat about him escape for the moment was impossible. He sensed
the growing pyramid of final retribution and began to formulate plans
whereby the mantle of responsibility might be transferred to other
aspiring shoulders.

The cumulative financial problem was a simple matter of geometrical
progression, at the far end of which lay a solution consisting of
several quarts of blood. He faced a wire-edged razor, seeking a
gilt-edged dodge, and so far his brain had failed to formulate the safe
way out.

His attempts at transferring the long end of the load to the strutting
deppities who hung around the Temple of Luck met with less success.
"Long as you stays Soopreem enough to wrassle wid de financial
department, us leaves you run it. You is soopreem now. Stay dat way."

Later on Brother Livingstone approached Honey Tone and warned the
leader to stay Soopreem or pay the charges on one life-size mistake.
"Confidential like, Honey Tone, I tells you stay soopreem o' else tell
de grave committee de facts fo' yo' tombstone."

The person of the Soopreem Leader became the object of watchful care on
the part of three shifts of Deppity Gardeens. Day and night there were
two or three watchful waiters on the job.

The fourth pay day was approaching and with it an obligation to pay out more than four thousand dollars. Receipts were falling off. On Wednesday night Honey Tone's bankroll audited less than three thousand dollars. He tried to split the pot with the Deppity Gardeens in return for liberty. In this he failed.

On Thursday night, as near as he could see, all the gates were closed. He was on a one-way road.

CHAPTER XIX

1.

> "All I does is follow mah feet,
> 'Ceptin' when de boss says, 'Stop an' eat!'
> Follow mah feet de whole day through;
> Follow mah feet 'till I burns a shoe,
> Shovin' a truck load o' po'k an' beans,
> Loadin' de boat fo' New O'leans."

Back of his truck on the dock the Wildcat set the pace for his fellows. The man in front of him found the Wildcat forever at his heels. The man following had a hard time keeping up.

Now and then the Wildcat's feet abandoned the steady trot for a gait which included considerable prancing, embellished with a new series of fancy steps, limited only by the inertia of the freight truck with which the stepper's ambition was retarded.

"On de down-hill drag let yo' hind legs slide;
Mawnin', Mistah Debbil, git aboa'd an' ride.
Git behin' me, Satan, on de up-hill road,
I'se a one-horse sinner wid a two-horse load."

Late in the afternoon the Wildcat's tactics had converted a group of admirers who had discovered in the prosaic business of rustling freight a first-class chance to make a laughing game of it. Meanwhile, they were moving record tonnage.

At evening the pier foreman sent for the Wildcat. "Tomorrow morning you take a gang down to Section Seventeen and start moving flour into the West King. There'll be five a day extra in it--that'll buy grub for the goat."

"Cap'n, yessuh--you means I'se fo'man?"

"That's what I mean. Keep your niggers rustlin'."

"Yass suh! Sho' will!" The Wildcat jerked at Lily's string halter. "Goat, say you'se 'bliged to de cap'n. Stan' roun' theh, fo' I shows you who's de boss wid a club!"

"Blaaa!" returned Lily.

The pier foreman smiled. "You might round up some more men if you can find 'em," he continued. "We can use a lot more. I'll give you twenty dollars a man for all you can get. Tell 'em ten a day, with grub and quarters furnished here on the dock."

"Cap'n, you means I gits twenty dollars fo' ev'y stevedo' nigger whut I 'cumulates?"

"That's it."

"How much is a hund'ed niggers, suh?"

"Two thousand dollars."

"Cap'n, you gits 'em tomorr'. Us kin rule dat many single handed--me 'suadin' an' Lily rammin'. Mebbe two hund'ed. Come on heah, goat! Le's go!"

The Wildcat left the pier with visions of a military formation of a million men, marching steadily toward a place where they were worth twenty dollars apiece to him. In his dream of being king of all labour agents he failed to include the difficulties with which his pathway was beset. The stevedores' strike, gaining strength each day, now included a floating committee whose duty it was to discourage the enlistment of new labour.

The Wildcat borrowed a dollar and ate supper at the lunch counter where he had met Trombone, hoping that he might again encounter that individual. Ranged about him were ten or fifteen hearty eaters; and to this group, at the termination of his own meal, he addressed his invitation to participate in the business of loading steamships with outbound freight. "Ten dollahs a day, boy, comf'table place fo' sleepin', an' all de grub you kin eat."

His oration fell on barren ground. He left the lunch counter without having gained a single recruit. "C'm on heah, Lily. Dese city niggers sho' is triflin'. Whut us needs is fiel' han's, o' else some heavy 'suader like a hoe handle. Us aims to sleep some now. Mebbe tomorr' Lady Luck boons me wid men whut craves a job wid rations an' ten dollahs a day."

For a while the next morning the work of loading the West King with flour lagged a little under the direction of the new foreman. At eleven o'clock, noting the epidemic of reluctance to move out of a slow drag which had afflicted his gang, the Wildcat climbed to the top of a tier of flour barrels. He took out his knife and whittled through the hoops of a barrel. He resumed his place on the pier. "Break down dat top line. Git movin'! Haul out 'at bottom bar'l! Stan' back when dey comes!"

They came. An avalanche of rolling barrels rolled wildly across the deck of the pier. The top one on which the hoops were cut landed with a smash in the centre of an explosive spray of flour. The atmosphere was suddenly white dust.... Black complexions presently became grey.

Perspiring freight jugglers began to laugh at their fellows. In three minutes the roof of the pier was echoing back the volleys of high-pitched laughter which lifted from below. Until noon, and then through the long afternoon, all that the Wildcat's men did was to laugh their heads off at the slightest provocation and move more freight than the ship's cargo booms could handle.

> "Ah likes biscuits an' Ah likes bread,
> Doan' like 'em plastered on mah head,
> Craves to have 'em spread around on mah inside,
> 'Sted of havin' dough a-drippin' off mah hide."

The pier foreman, passing the Wildcat's crew late in the afternoon, paused to look the deal over. "Everything all right?"

"Cap'n, yessuh. Dey's good boys. 'Clined to mope some at fust, but dey got laughin' some way. Since den dey's been movin' 'long."

Without knowing it, the Wildcat had mixed the essence of all the theories of efficiency into one barrel of flour. The results of the administered dose were showing on the tally boards in the freight office at the end of the long pier. The transportation superintendent sent for the pier foreman. "Jim, who is handling the flour into the West King?"

"Young nigger called Wildcat--right name is Marsden. Got him yesterday."

"Keep him forever. The Empire docks tomorrow for a mixed cargo for New Orleans. Sixteen thousand tons. Let this Wildcat boy handle all of it--as long as he lasts."

2.

On Friday morning Honey Tone groaned himself awake, realizing when his eyes were open that less than thirty-six hours lay between his fragile form and blood-tinted trouble. It seemed to him that his self-appointed guardians clung closer with the passage of the hours, as if they suspected their soopreem treasury of perfecting a plot which might include his exit. The obligations of the moment were four thousand dollars, and in Honey Tone's bulging pocket but three-fourths of that amount awaited the pay hour which would come with Saturday night.

Saturday dawned, and with it the sprout of an idea had shoved through the graveyard ground of Honey Tone's dejection. In mournful tones, hardly hoping that success would attend his latest scheme, he announced it to his guardian deppities. "Brethren, yo' leadeh's efforts has been rewarded like de oil in de widow's croose. F'm now on us pays back de original 'scription wid a hund'ed per cent intres', an'--hearkin' unto dese words--oveh an' above de 'riginal an' de intres', a bonus equal to de 'vestment! Doan ask what de Lawd means when de blessin' showers down. Git in de rain an' git wet wid cash. Th'ee fo' one--dat's whut pays!"

At evening, before he took his place at the pay table, he repeated the announcement. The rooms of the Temple were crowded and the flock was silent, hanging with acute interest on the Soopreemest's words. Honey Tone held up his hand. He bowed right and left, and the glittering tinsel on the mandarin cap reflected the colour of minted gold from the yellow lights. He held aloft the hilt of the gilded sword that swung from his yellow belt. He sheathed his sword and parked his nervous left hand in the folds of the yellow sash that draped across his chest. "Brethren ob de Temple: Sow an' reap. As you sows, you likewise reaps. De Goddess of Gold, an' de lady's husban' ol' man Midas, has smiled agin upon ou' humble efforts. Tonight Ah makes a momentous announcement befo' Ah returns wid intres' de 'vestments you made las' week. Up to now de 'financial repayments has been two fo' one. F'm now on us pays twice dat much!"

He paused to let his words sink in. "Fo' eve'y dollah you 'vests you gits de dollah back, anotheh dollah for intres', an', as a special bonus, anotheh dollah whut makes de th'ee fo' one. Dis Special 'Vestment Depahtment is open now an' will be run wid de lef han' whilst de right, not knowin' whut de lef' han' does, pays out yo' las' week's cash. Fawm in line. Ah pays an' receives at de same table. Who is de fust brotheh? Yass indeed! Heah's yo' money--an' you says you craves to 'vest it in de th'ee fo' one fund. Praise de Lawd! De los' sheep sees de light."

Some there were who failed to see the light, but by strenuous persuasion Honey Tone managed to reclaim enough of his payments to piece out the missing thousand.

Over and above the success he enjoyed in keeping his epidermis free from the parked razors of revenge, he pouched a few hundred dollars' surplus before the hour of payment ceased. With it, including the borrowed and juggled thousand, he had incurred an obligation to repay another staggering sum on the following Saturday night.

Thankful for his escape from the crisis of the moment and a little bit shaken by the acute peril which had confronted him, he sat heavily at the pay table, and sagged down in his soopreem robes. He ran his eye over the pay list, and for the first time he noticed an unpaid investor. "Pike Canfield--$100.00."

A knock sounded at the outer door. The outer guard clattered in. "Brotheh Canfield, an' a strange brotheh who desires to be led straight."

"Tell Brotheh Canfield to enteh unto de Soopreem presence," Honey Tone returned, according to the ritual. Then, under his breath, "Dam 'at Trombone nigger. How come he so promp' at de las' minute?"

CHAPTER XX

1.

A little late at the Sutter Street lunch counter by reason of his added responsibilities at the dock, the Wildcat had found his friend Trombone impatiently awaiting him.

"Wilecat, does us miss de meetin' Ah loses a hund'ed dollahs. Grab yo' vittles an' eat on de run!"

"Whut time is you due at de Temple?"

"De meetin' done stahted a houah back--'less us gits dah in fifteen minnits de do's closed."

"Trombone, us has plenty ob time. Ah 'sorbs mah nutriment in five minnits--'at leaves ten fo' de trip. Ain't et me nothin' all day, 'ceptin' breakfus' an' some san'wiches at noon time. Sho' been busy loadin' de ol' Empire fo' N'Awl'uns. Dey made me de gang boss--I'se got mo' niggers dan ol' cunnel had in de Fust Service Battalion. Sho' is busy. Niggers craves to mope--ah un-craves 'em like de Lootenant used to--gits 'em all laffin' so ha'd dey forgits de wuk. Fo' long dey ain't no mo' w'uk, an' eve'ybody feels noble. Dat's all de talk--heah's mah ham, sizzlin' in de gravy.... Stan' up heah, Lily; eat dese lettuce greens."

The Wildcat did an hour's eating in three minutes. "Whuf--ol' rations sho' tastes noble. Whah at's yo' soopreem ol' leadeh whut pays out de money? Ah craves to 'vest some mahse'f. Tonight I has money. Las' week me an' Lily was bust. Le's go!"

Ten minutes later Trombone and the Wildcat, leading Lily, were at the outer door of the Temple of Luck. There followed the ritual business of three knocks and the ceremony of admittance.

2.

Honey Tone saw the Wildcat one second before that individual saw the Soopreem paymaster. One second was enough for Honey Tone. In his brain was born a scheme whereby the heavy mantle of leadership, including the ponderous pyramid of financial obligations, might be shifted to the Wildcat's shoulders. He got up from his throne at the paytable and plowed his way toward the Wildcat. He held out the hand of fellowship. "Wilecat, how is you? How is de Worshupful Potentate f'm de distant lan'?"

"Honey Tone! Honey Tone Boone! How come you heah?"

Honey Tone took the Wildcat by the arm. "Brothehs, in de humble yaller raiment of a plain nigger de long-looked-fo' Barzil Leadeh has come to 'scort you all to de promis' lan'."

He half dragged the Wildcat to a little room opening off the larger hall, and thereafter for five minutes Honey Tone used some private eloquence on his old-time acquaintance. The Soopreem Leader took pains to omit the detail covering the four-thousand-dollar obligation that went with the job. Finally the Wildcat weakened. "Sho' sounds noble, Honey Tone. Tell me de res'."

"You is de head boss ob de New Worl' Af'ican Colony, an' weahs de robes," Honey Tone concluded. "You is Temp'rary Soopreem Leadeh ob de Temple whilst I 'tends to some private business a sho't ways out ob town. When de Barzil Colony is runnin' you gits de job ob Soopreem King. All you does now is keep yo' mouth shut an' look soopreem. Dis steamboatin' you says you is 'gaged in comes in handy. You tells de membehs at de propeh time dat you is loadin' de boat fo' de Barzil Colony."

Honey Tone left his convert and prepared the way for the transition with the assembled audience.

Half way through his discourse he was interrupted by Trombone Pike, who craved to get his hundred dollars before the flight of Honey Tone's imagination lifted the soopreem one above paltry things like financial obligations. Honey Tone paid him with three quick movements--a dig for the roll, an outstretching of a handful of cash, and the grip of eternal brotherhood. "'At's dat. Dah you is."

Meanwhile the Wildcat's languid brain had stumbled over an idea as big as a church. "Ah leads de brethren to de dock--an' gits twenty dollahs fo' every man!" When Honey Tone returned, the Wildcat eagerly succumbed to the role imposed on him. "Sho' kin, Honey Tone. Sho' glad to be Temp'rary Soopreem Leadeh. Ah learns dese brethren de steamboat bizness. Sho' glad to show 'em all I knows an' git 'em stahted."

"Wait heah till I 'suades 'em to let you handle everything." Honey Tone left the Wildcat alone for the second time and made a further announcement to the brethren. "De Wo'shipful Temp'rary Soopreem Leadeh suggests, wid de high knowledge he has fo' suggestin', dat if he has de treasury department in his han's de payments on 'vestments will increase up to fo' to one. Dat alone shows you whut a big man he is. Nex' week he pays you all yo' 'vestments, intres' at a hund'ed per cent, a bonus ob de same amount, an' a special dividend equal to one an' all. Ah hereby 'spectfully resigns de robes ob office, an' names a 'nishiation c'mmittee ob twelve brothehs to 'dorn de new Soopreem Temp'rary Leadeh wid de raiment of his rank."

Honey Tone returned to the Wildcat. "You's been 'lected unan'mous. De 'nitiation cer'monies is ready. You gits de Gran' Degree right away. Heah's de treasury. Ain't no bills due--yet. Don't owe nuthin'."

Honey Tone split his roll, being burdened with the rudiments of the principle of safety first. He shoved the money at the Wildcat and hurried the candidate to the door before the victim had a chance to count the cash.

There followed an impromptu initiation ceremony, interrupted but once by Lily's bleating, after which the Wildcat realized that he was the head of something that he knew mighty little about. He looked around for Honey Tone, seeking the moral support that might derive from the presence of his old friend and enemy.

Honey Tone had explained himself loose from his guards. Honey Tone was gone.

The Wildcat fumbled around with some oversized words, and then the real object of his speech came to him. "Dese niggers means twenty dollahs apiece--on de dock." He launched into a wild description of the New World African Colony. He pictured a life of ease in which each charter member of the colony who believed in heaven would be reluctant to trade heaven for a stevedore's career. He added the time phrase which was the essence of the whole affair. "You meets me heah tomorr' mawnin' at six o'clock. Ah leads you to de boat whah you sees how fas' kin' you git de freight aboa'd. So as yo' gits de wages yo' labour is worthy ob, like de Bible says, I 'ranges dat ev'y man gits ten dollahs a day an' grub."

3.

Before the light of dawn began to chase the San Francisco fogs up the bay the charter members of the New World African Colony began to assemble at the gates of the Temple. When the Wildcat appeared at six o'clock he was greeted by more than two hundred worthy brethren, all of whom craved to learn the boat-loading business at ten dollars a day. He marched his gang to the Embarcadero, yelling orders in a manner that made some of the veterans of the A.E.F. homesick.

"Silence in de ranks!" The clamour subsided. "When Ah columns you lef', head fo' de big buildin'!" The big building was the entrance to the pier against which, eating charter money faster than the banks could loan it and hungry for her sixteen thousand tons of mixed freight, lay the Empire.

At half past seven the Wildcat reported to the pier foreman at the office in the end of the long building. "Cap'n, suh, heah's more'n two hund'ed twenty-dollah niggers. How much does dat come to, suh?"

The pier foreman ran his eye over the crowd without answering. He disappeared into the office, where he spoke quickly to his clerk. "Cut all the labour-grabbers off the payroll. Call 'em in. Here's more men than I've seen in a year."

Outside there began the brief business of distributing the new supply of much-needed labour. This accomplished, the Wildcat came in for his share of attention. "We can use another gang like this. Can you get 'em by tomorrow?"

"Cap'n, suh, Ah gits fo' times dis many does you crave 'em. When does Ah git de money?"

Fifteen minutes later the Wildcat received a piece of blue paper. "Cap'n, suh, Ah cain't read whut de papeh says. Kin you read fo' me, please, suh?"

"That's a check for four thousand and eighty dollars--two hundred and four men at twenty a throw."

"Lawd gawd, Lady Luck, you sho' showered down dis time!" The Wildcat's brain could surround the eighty-dollar part, but the four-thousand end was something not yet real. He stowed the check in his pocket with the fragment of the treasury roll of the Temple of Luck.

On Saturday, unable to restrain his anxiety to see what so much money looked like, he persuaded the pier foreman to send the clerk to the bank to get the check cashed. The cash was handed to the Wildcat. He stowed it away in various pockets of the yaller suit. "Ol' money sticks out like a stole chicken. Neveh did see so much money."

That night, under the stress of prosperity, the Wildcat quit an hour early. He drifted to the Temple of Luck, intending to sit easy and smoke a cigar and talk big talk to the evening assembly of brethren. Two or three of Honey Tone's former guardians were busy loafing at the Temple when the Wildcat arrived. After a period of silence, following the salutations appropriate for the Soopreem Leader, a deppity led up to the matter of meeting the financial obligations which fell due that evening. "Ah figgehs, Soopreem, dat dey's somethin' like fo' thousan' dollahs to be paid out tonight. Sho' is a lot o' money."

The Wildcat was interested. "Fo' thousan'? Whah at is de money comin' f'm?"

Five anxious brethren sat up. It was all right for the Soopreem Leadeh to enjoy himself on whatever subject pleased him, as long as there were no personal dollar signs attached to the subject.

"You knows whah it comes f'm. You's jokin', Soopreem! Go 'long wid yo' talk. 'Scuse me fo' speakin' so familiah, but de money question sho' is in de fust rank. Specially since you pays fo' to one. De Pas' Soopreem Leadeh strained hisse'f to pay th'ee fo' one."

In the course of the next five minutes the Wildcat's eyes were opened concerning the generous ease with which Honey Tone had relinquished what appeared to be a position of prominence second to none for social and political status. He sought to make his escape, only to discover the same restraint which had defeated Honey Tone's plans of flight.

"Come easy--go easy." The Wildcat surrendered to the clutch of circumstance. He felt the diminishing weight of the four thousand dollars. "Ah kep' it a week--dat's longeh den Ah eveh had such big money befo'! Now Ah has to buy mahse'f free wid it, 'stead ob usin' it fo' rations an' sech. Doggone! Whah at is Lady Luck?"

The hour for the meeting came. The Wildcat adorned himself with his soopreem robes. He cut a long end from the yaller sash and tied it around the mascot's stomach. "Heah, goat, doggone you. Git ca'm. Stan' still till Ah adorns yo' wid de soopreem belly band. See kin you make Lady Luck heah you. Dat woman sho' fo'got mah name."

"Blaaa!" Festooned with the yellow sash, Lily did the best she could to make Lady Luck respond, but Lady Luck was deaf.

Lady Luck was A.W.O.L. Thereafter for an hour the Wildcat sat at the Soopreem table, watching his stack of greenbacks melt out before him on four-to-one obligations incurred by the absent Honey Tone.

For a while, with every disappearing dollar, the Wildcat mentally showered the absent Honey Tone with epithets picked up during overstressed moments of an active life. Then to the Temp'rary Soopreem Leader's mind there came a faint resolve to try the ultimate arrow of his pack in an effort to reclaim his melting money. "De clickers!"

At the conclusion of his misery he made an announcement covering the programme of an attempt to defeat the evil which had run him down.

He stood up on the chair where he had been sitting. "Brethren, befo' us gits too deep into de evenin' us devotes a social hour to Lady Luck. Count off into squads, dig deep in yo' raiment fo' ammunition an' de clickin' weapons, den for'd march--into de battle whah de top sides means vick'ry o' else de grave-diggin' squad! Afteh de squad leadehs decides who is de bes' man, as yo' Soopreem Leadeh I claims de priv'lege o' meetin' de victors on de clickin' fiel' of battle. Dat's all. Git faded an' shoot fas'."

A battle royal. Thereafter for half an hour the air was thick with prayer. Presently most of the four thousand had been prayed into the hands of half a dozen squad leaders.

Then the Wildcat spoke. "Winners! Lady Luck sho' smiled down on you. Now your Soopreem Leadeh makes 'at woman laff at you. Stan' by me, Lily!"

The mascot goat bleated her message of encouragement. Spectators rallied around. Out of his left shoe the Wildcat hauled his personal weapons. On the floor before him he cast the last fragment of his four-thousand-dollar roll. In the narrow circle of victors exploded his point-blank challenge.

"Shoots a hund'ed! Shower down. Ah craves action!

> "You neveh kin tell till de gallopers stop
> Whut de numbehs reads dat lays on top.
> Comin' out a top side seven or 'leven
> Is Wilecat talk fo' a payday heaven.
> Seven's a winner when it shows up fust,
> But afteh yo' point a seven means bust.
> Comin' out fust wid a dooce, twelve, o' trey
> Is jes' like throwin' yo' money away,
> 'Cept you keeps de dice an' stahts once mo'
> By layin' yo' money on de gam'lin' flo'.
> Suppose you releases a fo', six, eight,
> You tries yo' bes' to duplicate.

De same hol's true fo' a five, nine, ten,
But a seven's boun' to git you now an' then.
As I said befo' does a seven come fust
Befo' you makes yo' point, it means you's bust."

In fifteen minutes six ex-victors had joined the circle of innocent
bystanders and were hunting for phrases to explain to themselves just
how it happened. The Wildcat, stowing away the incoming money with his
left hand, swept his victorious right high above his head. In his moist
palm nestled his pussonal dice.

"I lets it lay. Shoots it all!"

"Ain't got dat much." The last man was suffering from reduced
circumstances.

"How much is you? Shoots de fifty! I'se faded. Gallopers, stan' by me!
Stay soopreem. Bam! An' I reads, six-ace. Deppity--you's done!"

The Wildcat, perspiring copiously in his official robes of supremacy,
got to his feet. He parked the gallopers in his inside pocket. He
reached for Lily's leading string. "Brethren--me an' Lily stahted
soopreem when we come heah. Dat's de way we finishes. I bids you--good
night!"

4.

With Lily at his heels, the favourite of Lady Luck made his way into
the midnight fog which lay above the city. He walked to Market Street,
and at the ferry building he headed down the Embarcadero toward the
pier where the Empire was loading. In the deep shadows cast by a post
in the long pier he removed his trailing robe. He rolled his insignia

under his arm. Under the arc lights along the pier the men of the night shift were rustling the last of the freight to the Empire's side.

With Lily at his heels, the Wildcat went aboard the ship. The officer on watch recognized him. "What you doin' out so late, boy? Thought you run the day shift?"

"Cap'n,--yessuh,--I does. Me an' Lily was projectin' roun' some. Us ain't got no place to go."

The Wildcat lingered on this last statement. "No place to go." Then he summoned courage enough to voice a request which expressed a longing that had developed since he had first known the Empire's destination.

"Cap'n, suh," he said slowly, "kin me an' Lily ride wid you to New Awl'uns?--Us craves to git south."

"I'll say you can. We need about nine good waiters for the trip."

"Cap'n, suh, dat's me! When us starts I'se de same as nine."

"You're hired. Sign on tomorrow."

In his eagerness the Wildcat jerked heavily at Lily's leading string. "Come on heah, goat, le's git down in de ol' boat's cellar whah de kitchen is an' git to work. Say you's 'bliged to de cap'n."

"Blaaa!" Lily voiced her gratitude.

On the third deck down, the Wildcat tied Lily to a stanchion. He threw his official costume on the deck in front of the mascot goat.

"See kin you eat dis soopreem raiment. Us is done bein' soopreem. Hot dam! New Awl'uns boun'! Den Memphis--dat's home!"

The Wildcat felt the thick packages of bank notes in the inside pockets of his yaller suit. "Sho' big money. Money--dis time stan' by me."

"I kin ride a steamboat--I don' pay no fare,
I kin ride a steamboat--anywhere.
Dat's de reason I'se as happy as a bee,
Me an' Lily's Memphis boun'--Memphis, Ten-o-see."

The Codes Of Hammurabi And Moses
W. W. Davies

QTY

The discovery of the Hammurabi Code is one of the greatest achievements of archaeology, and is of paramount interest, not only to the student of the Bible, but also to all those interested in ancient history...

Religion   **ISBN: *1-59462-338-4***   **Pages:132**
MSRP $12.95

The Theory of Moral Sentiments
Adam Smith

QTY

This work from 1749. contains original theories of conscience amd moral judgment and it is the foundation for systemof morals.

Philosophy **ISBN: *1-59462-777-0***   **Pages:536**
MSRP $19.95

Jessica's First Prayer
Hesba Stretton

QTY

In a screened and secluded corner of one of the many railway-bridges which span the streets of London there could be seen a few years ago, from five o'clock every morning until half past eight, a tidily set-out coffee-stall, consisting of a trestle and board, upon which stood two large tin cans, with a small fire of charcoal burning under each so as to keep the coffee boiling during the early hours of the morning when the work-people were thronging into the city on their way to their daily toil...

Pages:84

Childrens   **ISBN: *1-59462-373-2***   **MSRP $9.95**

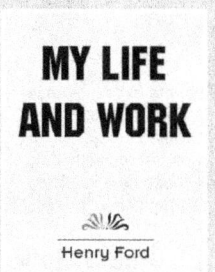

My Life and Work
Henry Ford

QTY

Henry Ford revolutionized the world with his implementation of mass production for the Model T automobile. Gain valuable business insight into his life and work with his own auto-biography... "We have only started on our development of our country we have not as yet, with all our talk of wonderful progress, done more than scratch the surface. The progress has been wonderful enough but..."

Pages:300

Biographies/   **ISBN: *1-59462-198-5***   **MSRP $21.95**

www.bookjungle.com *email: sales@bookjungle.com fax: 630-214-0564 mail: Book Jungle PO Box 2226 Champaign, IL 61825*

The Art of Cross-Examination
Francis Wellman

QTY

I presume it is the experience of every author, after his first book is published upon an important subject, to be almost overwhelmed with a wealth of ideas and illustrations which could readily have been included in his book, and which to his own mind, at least, seem to make a second edition inevitable. Such certainly was the case with me; and when the first edition had reached its sixth impression in five months, I rejoiced to learn that it seemed to my publishers that the book had met with a sufficiently favorable reception to justify a second and considerably enlarged edition. ..

Pages:412

Reference   ISBN: *1-59462-647-2*   *MSRP $19.95*

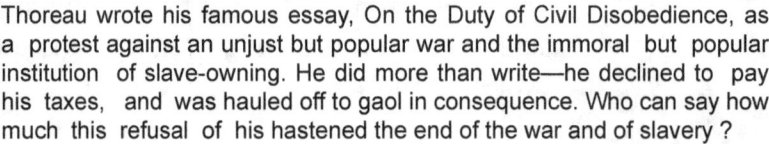

On the Duty of Civil Disobedience
Henry David Thoreau

QTY

Thoreau wrote his famous essay, On the Duty of Civil Disobedience, as a protest against an unjust but popular war and the immoral but popular institution of slave-owning. He did more than write—he declined to pay his taxes, and was hauled off to gaol in consequence. Who can say how much this refusal of his hastened the end of the war and of slavery ?

Law   ISBN: *1-59462-747-9*   **Pages:48**

MSRP $7.45

Dream Psychology Psychoanalysis for Beginners
Sigmund Freud

QTY

Sigmund Freud, born Sigismund Schlomo Freud (May 6, 1856 - September 23, 1939), was a Jewish-Austrian neurologist and psychiatrist who co-founded the psychoanalytic school of psychology. Freud is best known for his theories of the unconscious mind, especially involving the mechanism of repression; his redefinition of sexual desire as mobile and directed towards a wide variety of objects; and his therapeutic techniques, especially his understanding of transference in the therapeutic relationship and the presumed value of dreams as sources of insight into unconscious desires.

Pages:196

Psychology   ISBN: *1-59462-905-6*   *MSRP $15.45*

The Miracle of Right Thought
Orison Swett Marden

QTY

Believe with all of your heart that you will do what you were made to do. When the mind has once formed the habit of holding cheerful, happy, prosperous pictures, it will not be easy to form the opposite habit. It does not matter how improbable or how far away this realization may see, or how dark the prospects may be, if we visualize them as best we can, as vividly as possible, hold tenaciously to them and vigorously struggle to attain them, they will gradually become actualized, realized in the life. But a desire, a longing without endeavor, a yearning abandoned or held indifferently will vanish without realization.

Pages:360

Self Help   ISBN: *1-59462-644-8*   *MSRP $25.45*

QTY

The Rosicrucian Cosmo-Conception Mystic Christianity by *Max Heindel*   ISBN: *1-59462-188-8* **$38.95**
The Rosicrucian Cosmo-conception is not dogmatic, neither does it appeal to any other authority than the reason of the student. It is: not controversial, but is: sent forth in the, hope that it may help to clear...   New Age/Religion Pages 646

Abandonment To Divine Providence by *Jean-Pierre de Caussade*   ISBN: *1-59462-228-0* **$25.95**
"The Rev. Jean Pierre de Caussade was one of the most remarkable spiritual writers of the Society of Jesus in France in the 18th Century. His death took place at Toulouse in 1751. His works have gone through many editions and have been republished...   Inspirational/Religion Pages 400

Mental Chemistry by *Charles Haanel*   ISBN: *1-59462-192-6* **$23.95**
Mental Chemistry allows the change of material conditions by combining and appropriately utilizing the power of the mind. Much like applied chemistry creates something new and unique out of careful combinations of chemicals the mastery of mental chemistry...   New Age Pages 354

The Letters of Robert Browning and Elizabeth Barret Barrett 1845-1846 vol II   ISBN: *1-59462-193-4* **$35.95**
by *Robert Browning* and *Elizabeth Barrett*   Biographies Pages 596

Gleanings In Genesis (volume I) by *Arthur W. Pink*   ISBN: *1-59462-130-6* **$27.45**
Appropriately has Genesis been termed "the seed plot of the Bible" for in it we have, in germ form, almost all of the great doctrines which are afterwards fully developed in the books of Scripture which follow...   Religion/Inspirational Pages 420

The Master Key by *L. W. de Laurence*   ISBN: *1-59462-001-6* **$30.95**
In no branch of human knowledge has there been a more lively increase of the spirit of research during the past few years than in the study of Psychology, Concentration and Mental Discipline. The requests for authentic lessons in Thought Control, Mental Discipline and...   New Age/Business Pages 422

The Lesser Key Of Solomon Goetia by *L. W. de Laurence*   ISBN: *1-59462-092-X* **$9.95**
This translation of the first book of the "Lernegton" which is now for the first time made accessible to students of Talismanic Magic was done, after careful collation and edition, from numerous Ancient Manuscripts in Hebrew, Latin, and French...   New Age/Occult Pages 92

Rubaiyat Of Omar Khayyam by *Edward Fitzgerald*   ISBN: *1-59462-332-5* **$13.95**
Edward Fitzgerald, whom the world has already learned, in spite of his own efforts to remain within the shadow of anonymity, to look upon as one of the rarest poets of the century, was born at Bredfield, in Suffolk, on the 31st of March, 1809. He was the third son of John Purcell...   Music Pages 172

Ancient Law by *Henry Maine*   ISBN: *1-59462-128-4* **$29.95**
The chief object of the following pages is to indicate some of the earliest ideas of mankind, as they are reflected in Ancient Law, and to point out the relation of those ideas to modern thought.   Religion/History Pages 452

Far-Away Stories by *William J. Locke*   ISBN: *1-59462-129-2* **$19.45**
"Good wine needs no bush, but a collection of mixed vintages does. And this book is just such a collection. Some of the stories I do not want to remain buried for ever in the museum files of dead magazine-numbers an author's not unpardonable vanity..."   Fiction Pages 272

Life of David Crockett by *David Crockett*   ISBN: *1-59462-250-7* **$27.45**
"Colonel David Crockett was one of the most remarkable men of the times in which he lived. Born in humble life, but gifted with a strong will, an indomitable courage, and unremitting perseverance...   Biographies/New Age Pages 424

Lip-Reading by *Edward Nitchie*   ISBN: *1-59462-206-4* **$25.95**
Edward B. Nitchie, founder of the New York School for the Hard of Hearing, now the Nitchie School of Lip-Reading, Inc, wrote "LIP-READING Principles and Practice". The development and perfecting of this meritorious work on lip-reading was an undertaking...   How-to Pages 400

A Handbook of Suggestive Therapeutics, Applied Hypnotism, Psychic Science   ISBN: *1-59462-214-0* **$24.95**
by *Henry Munro*   Health/New Age/Health/Self-help Pages 376

A Doll's House: and Two Other Plays by *Henrik Ibsen*   ISBN: *1-59462-112-8* **$19.95**
Henrik Ibsen created this classic when in revolutionary 1848 Rome. Introducing some striking concepts in playwriting for the realist genre, this play has been studied the world over.   Fiction/Classics/Plays 308

The Light of Asia by *sir Edwin Arnold*   ISBN: *1-59462-204-3* **$13.95**
In this poetic masterpiece, Edwin Arnold describes the life and teachings of Buddha. The man who was to become known as Buddha to the world was born as Prince Gautama of India but he rejected the worldly riches and abandoned the reigns of power when...   Religion/History/Biographies Pages 170

The Complete Works of Guy de Maupassant by *Guy de Maupassant*   ISBN: *1-59462-157-8* **$16.95**
"For days and days, nights and nights, I had dreamed of that first kiss which was to consecrate our engagement, and I knew not on what spot I should put my lips..."   Fiction/Classics Pages 240

The Art of Cross-Examination by *Francis L. Wellman*   ISBN: *1-59462-309-0* **$26.95**
Written by a renowned trial lawyer, Wellman imparts his experience and uses case studies to explain how to use psychology to extract desired information through questioning.   How-to/Science/Reference Pages 408

Answered or Unanswered? by *Louisa Vaughan*   ISBN: *1-59462-248-5* **$10.95**
Miracles of Faith in China   Religion Pages 112

The Edinburgh Lectures on Mental Science (1909) by *Thomas*   ISBN: *1-59462-008-3* **$11.95**
This book contains the substance of a course of lectures recently given by the writer in the Queen Street Hall, Edinburgh. Its purpose is to indicate the Natural Principles governing the relation between Mental Action and Material Conditions...   New Age/Psychology Pages 148

Ayesha by *H. Rider Haggard*   ISBN: *1-59462-301-5* **$24.95**
Verily and indeed it is the unexpected that happens! Probably if there was one person upon the earth from whom the Editor of this, and of a certain previous history, did not expect to hear again...   Classics Pages 380

Ayala's Angel by *Anthony Trollope*   ISBN: *1-59462-352-X* **$29.95**
The two girls were both pretty, but Lucy who was twenty-one who supposed to be simple and comparatively unattractive, whereas Ayala was credited, as her Bombwhat romantic name might show, with poetic charm and a taste for romance. Ayala when her father died was nineteen...   Fiction Pages 484

The American Commonwealth by *James Bryce*   ISBN: *1-59462-286-8* **$34.45**
An interpretation of American democratic political theory. It examines political mechanics and society from the perspective of Scotsman James Bryce   Politics Pages 572

Stories of the Pilgrims by *Margaret P. Pumphrey*   ISBN: *1-59462-116-0* **$17.95**
This book explores pilgrims religious oppression in England as well as their escape to Holland and eventual crossing to America on the Mayflower, and their early days in New England...   History Pages 268

QTY

The Fasting Cure *by Sinclair Upton* ISBN: *1-59462-222-1* **$13.95**
In the Cosmopolitan Magazine for May, 1910, and in the Contemporary Review (London) for April, 1910, I published an article dealing with my experiences in fasting. I have written a great many magazine articles, but never one which attracted so much attention... New Age/Self Help/Health Pages 164

Hebrew Astrology *by Sepharial* ISBN: *1-59462-308-2* **$13.45**
In these days of advanced thinking it is a matter of common observation that we have left many of the old landmarks behind and that we are now pressing forward to greater heights and to a wider horizon than that which represented the mind-content of our progenitors... Astrology Pages 144

Thought Vibration or The Law of Attraction in the Thought World ISBN: *1-59462-127-6* **$12.95**
by William Walker Atkinson Psychology/Religion Pages 144

Optimism *by Helen Keller* ISBN: *1-59462-108-X* **$15.95**
Helen Keller was blind, deaf, and mute since 19 months old, yet famously learned how to overcome these handicaps, communicate with the world, and spread her lectures promoting optimism. An inspiring read for everyone... Biographies/Inspirational Pages 84

Sara Crewe *by Frances Burnett* ISBN: *1-59462-360-0* **$9.45**
In the first place, Miss Minchin lived in London. Her home was a large, dull, tall one, in a large, dull square, where all the houses were alike, and all the sparrows were alike, and where all the door-knockers made the same heavy sound... Childrens/Classic Pages 88

The Autobiography of Benjamin Franklin *by Benjamin Franklin* ISBN: *1-59462-135-7* **$24.95**
The Autobiography of Benjamin Franklin has probably been more extensively read than any other American historical work, and no other book of its kind has had such ups and downs of fortune. Franklin lived for many years in England, where he was agent... Biographies/History Pages 332

Name	
Email	
Telephone	
Address	
City, State ZIP	

☐ **Credit Card**   ☐ **Check / Money Order**

Credit Card Number	
Expiration Date	
Signature	

Please Mail to: Book Jungle
PO Box 2226
Champaign, IL 61825
or Fax to: 630-214-0564

ORDERING INFORMATION

web: *www.bookjungle.com*
email: *sales@bookjungle.com*
fax: *630-214-0564*
mail: *Book Jungle PO Box 2226 Champaign, IL 61825*
or PayPal *to sales@bookjungle.com*

Please contact us for bulk discounts

DIRECT-ORDER TERMS

**20% Discount if You Order
Two or More Books**
Free Domestic Shipping!
Accepted: Master Card, Visa,
Discover, American Express